HUM

BAWDY

&

BLUE

FROM
THE

ROB LITTLE

CELLAR

Foreword

In 1940, Rob was born in Cardiff. His grandfather was Scottish, but both of his parents were Welsh born. In 1940, his grandfather worked for the local council, on the roads, until his sacking for theft. It was no surprise to the family: at home, all the signs were there. In 1941, Hitler bombing all parts of industrialised Wales, the family moved into a cottage in his grandfather's home village of Dunrovin, to save the baby Rob; he to go on to greater glory as a humorous writer.

Rob spent most of his working life on ships. From 1961, he served in the British Merchant Navy, working as an electrician, travelling to those many faraway places with strange sounding names, faraway over the sea. Rob honed his chat up lines using outrageous patter, flirting with any Sheila or Judy, having girls chortling uncontrollably at his mirth.

Entertainment for ship's crews, whilst at sea, in those days, was listening to BBC broadcasts on short wave radio and the chronic, ear-offending squelch. Having the urine extracted by a fellow crewmember was an ever-present danger. Rob gained proficiency at that form of amusement.

Rob had a short spell in London's Met Police, but the call of the sea was strong. Rob succumbed to the call. Eventually, he took a job on ferries, sailing to Northern Ireland and the Continent.

Rob remained at sea until retirement with ill health in 1988. In 1989, Rob and his wife Patricia, known to regulars as The Dragon, were mine hosts of the White Hart Hotel, in Brewery Street, Dumfries. Rob created a popular music venue at The Hart, the venue attracted well-known bands such as UK Subs, The Crazy World of Arthur Brown, The Groundhogs,

Goggsie's Midnight Scunners and an array of talented and popular local groups. Rob encouraged the town's young musicians to form bands, to practise at the venue and perform gigs there.

Rob's customers knew of his love of humour. His Bawdy and Blue book of 50000 words has over 249 pages: laughableness, from Alpha to Omega.

The sale of Rob's books has raised money for ovarian cancer charities.

Rob is dedicating this book to all armed-service members who have manned up and might now be down on their luck. He will send a donation from each book sale to the charity Help for Heroes.

Books by this author.

The Life of Riley and his Troubles: set in Northern Ireland.

The Jock Connection on the Trail of the Comic Billy Bagman: set in London's Met Police.

Scratcher in the Wry: a short story book.

Amazon Books publish in hardback, paperback and digital forms.

JAPANESE WAXING EXPERIENCE

I was on holiday in Tokyo. Feeling a bit tense and lonely, needing a spot of pampering, I decided to experience the pleasures of a Japanese massage. The girl masseuse the massage parlour assigned to me was dressed in a colourful, silky kimono, was petite and lovely, about five feet four inches tall with black hair, dark, almond-shaped eyes and small breasts. She said, 'My name is Violet. I will look after you.' She spoke good English with the intonation of the comic's take off.

In her dainty hand, Violet held mine and led me into a dimly lit cubicle with a marble slab. Traditional music was quietly playing from a ceiling speaker. Violet pointed me the direction of the changing room and said, 'Remove all clothing,' and handed me a towel to wrap around my waist.

Naked on the slab, which was pleasantly warm, Violet massaged my shoulders, chest, arms, legs, abdomen and back, with warm, oriental oils, feeling for stress points and tight muscles with tenderness. She gently applied pressure to my inner thighs and my buttocks, lifting my scrotum out of the way of her probing fingers. I'm sure I nodded off during the pleasurable experience. When Violet was finished, she had me turn over and asked me, again in the comic's send up voice, 'You like now some waxing?'

I replied, 'No,' 'I'm quite happy with what you have done. I feel refreshed and relaxed.' It concerned me that she might have offered the much publicised 'happy ending' and how I might answer the question.

'But you should have the waxing,' she pleaded, 'It is very good and a nice experience for you. No hair will leave the body. This one time I will do for free for you.'

I relented. She was young and a very nice and accomplished masseuse. I trusted her. I said, 'Okay, I will have the waxing.'

Violet helped me sit up and dismount from the slab; then she quickly had me stand facing it, up close. Taking hold of my dick, she placed it on the slab and began massaging it lovingly with fragrant oil.

My dick grew somewhat.

Violet said, 'For the full, most enjoyable experience you must keep your eyes closed during the waxing. You must not open them until I am finished.'

I did not see her reach for, pick up and remove a plank of wood from the cavity secreted beneath the slab, but felt it as she laid it gently on top of my erect dick.

I imagined this scenario later. Violet, with an evil smirk, much like that last look on face of a hari-kari pilot as he crashed his warplane into the enemy battleship, produced a sledgehammer from the same secret cavity, raised it high and then propelled it downwards with force and unerring accuracy onto the plank.

To Violet's cry of, 'Tenno Heika Banzai,' Wax shot out of both ears!

THE APPOINTMENT

James had a haggard look about him as he sat in the surgery facing his doctor. Seated across the desk, the doctor had noted the dark circles around James's eyes. He hoped he could resolve James's problem. James looked worried. He said to James, 'What can I help you with today?'

'Doctor, I've problems at home, at work and I've personal problems as well,' James explained in hurried speech.

'Well,' the doctor said, 'relax, start at the top. Tell me your problems at home and let's see what we can do to alleviate them.'

James explained, 'When I get home from work, my wife is always lurking behind our front door naked. She grabs me and rushes me into the kitchen. I have to perform sex with her, doggy style, over the sink, while she prepares the potatoes and vegetables for dinner. She's sex mad.

'I often miss the kick-off of a premiership football match on TV. She insists on having sex twice between 7 and 8. We go to bed at 10 o'clock. I'm knackered. She insists on sex then. She says she cannot get to sleep without it. During the night, she kicks me to wakefulness 6 or 7 times. She tells me she cannot get back off to sleep until she has it. She's always gagging for it. I find my pyjamas undone, pulled down about my knees, her on top of me, draining my bollocks of their juices. Doctor, I can hardly drag my sorry arse from the bed most mornings.

I shower alone before breakfast; thankfully, the shower is too small for two. Then I go into the kitchen for breakfast. My wife is always waiting for me. She never dresses in a housecoat. She is always naked. She wants sex while she prepares my breakfast. Apparently, she cannot time an egg unless we're engaging in sex, doggy style, so she can watch the egg dancing in the pot, on the cooker ring, in the simmering water, for the requisite time. I don't like runny eggs. I've to hang in there for a full three and a half minutes. I'm pleased I don't like my eggs really hard-boiled and it's not a duck egg. I wouldn't have the energy for either of those.

'Wow!' said the doctor, 'you do have a problem. And you say you have issues at work. Tell me about them.'

James continued, 'My boss at work is a woman. She's also sex mad, a nymphomaniac. As soon as I enter the office, she makes an excuse to see me for a morning conference. As soon as the door to the conference suite closes behind us, she trips me, pushes me to the floor, clambers on top of me, rips all my clothes off and has her way with me. I've to have five conferences with her each working a day. When I arrive at work, 10 o'clock tea break, 1 o'clock lunchtime, 3 o'clock coffee break, then before I leave for home. Each time, I have to allow her to assault me, literally rape me, on threat of the sack!'

'Your story is totally unbelievable, extraordinary,' the doctor said, furrowing his brow, 'it's probably why you look worn out. I certainly would not have the stamina to undergo your level of sexual encounters. Surely, your personal problems cannot be as bad as your sexual ones.

'They are, doctor, James said, 'I keep getting these terrible migraines every time I have a wank!

HISTORY LESSON

The main shopping street in my hometown climbs steeply for a furlong. A weathered, sandstone plinth marks the high-end of the street, where a bronze statue of an antlered stag stands rampant, its nostrils flaring, its eyes glaring madly. Beneath the bridge, at the lower end of the street, the river flows between grassy banks and, occasionally floods, into car parks and along other adjacent streets.

Credulous yesteryear townsfolk believed that the stag clambered down from its plinth every midnight, pranced down the street to the river, had a sniff around and a piddle there, then returned to the plinth. Early town scrolls suggest this myth was the main factor motivating those old townies to name the thoroughfare, Buck Loo Street.

Local historians suggest a local Duke changed the spelling to Buccleuch Street.

CHANCE MEETING ON BUCCLEUCH STREET

That Friday morning, looking for clothing suitable to wear whilst cruising on the vessel of a posh cruise company, I walked along Buchleuch Street. On the pavement outside a draper's doorway of the specialist store to which I was heading, I spotted an erstwhile mate of mine, "Wee Jock Laurie". Jock was standing stooped, bawling his eyes out, his feet slopping about in a pool of his own blood. Droplets from a haemorrhage, falling steadily from beneath his flowing raincoat, were adding to the pool, ripples spreading circularly across its surface. Other shoppers just passed by this ragged, dishevelled and obviously distressed, horizontally challenged man, averting their eyes.

They were bastards: Jock was an old mate who had often loaned me the price of a pint of beer when I was skint. I just had to act. Being outside the prestigious store, I began by asking genteelly, 'Jock, what in heaven's name is the matter?' Taking a step back after my enquiry, I tried to assess Jock's problem for myself.

'I've caught my foreskin up in my zip,' he told me between the heart wrenching sobs and the drawn-out, high-pitched squeals he let out when he inched his body towards the erect position and looked up at me, 'and the agony's killing me.'

Jock was ghostly white, blue of lips and sweat flowed freely from his brow; he was displaying the classic symptoms of shock.

Sensing he was unable to help himself and that he might bleed to death, I rushed through the draper's swing doors, throwing them back to their stops, and entered the store, resolved to seek help.

Hurriedly, I skirted displays of gent's shirts, squinted quickly at the suits and dinner jackets, and found the nearest counter. A tall, lanky girl, standing poised at the till, was dressed in an apron of the establishment. She smiled readily in my direction and revealed, through over-rouged lips, an empty space once filled by an upper-front incisor.

Focusing on the toothless gap, images of the entrance to Fingal's Cave sprung into my mind. The cruise was circuiting Scotland and sailing past some interesting, historic and picturesque islands. I wondered if I would see the cave as we sailed by the southern tip of Staffa. Perhaps we would anchor, the ship's crew lowering tenders from their derricks, allowing fee-paying cruisers a closer view. My thoughts had strayed to what use the girl could employ the gap: like gripping a pickled onion, holding, rotating and stripping it layer by layer.

The girl displayed the eagerness of the first-day shop assistant and her willingness to serve me was clear. 'Quick,' I ejaculated, 'can you give me something with which I can dress a prick?'

'Sorry, I tried, but the shop cannot help you,' I said to Jock, as I appeared in front of him dressed in a Batman outfit.

HEALTH WARNING

The Brighton Advertiser article today suggests replacing only 2% of your feeding requirements with a dried seaweed product will bring down your flatulent gas emissions by 99% within 72 days and help save the planet from global warming. As a major gas contributor to the atmosphere, you should have a crack at this and consider seeking out this product to the benefit of the planet and us all.

Let me assure you, though I feel there's no need for me to do so, that seaweed products have been a part of my healthy diet since birth and that I have never been flatulent, silently, uproariously loud or have ever given the impression that rats have crawled up my arse and died.

Confirmation of your dedication to this new diet regime will be evident when we next meet: you will have a healthier complexion and have more friends.

THE TRANSPLANT

Chuck was desperate to marry Betty, his beloved. However, he had a problem to redress before he could pop the question: he had a small dick. Chuck made an appointment with dick doctor, Doctor Dick Bigg-Widdler, to seek a remedy.

Doctor Dick Bigg-Widdler examined Chuck's dick and said, 'In the past, I've been able to work miracles with earplug-sized dicks. I regularly offer patients two treatments. I have had no failures,' ejaculated Doctor Dick Bigg-Widdler, 'I can place a hollow, extendable pipe within your dick shaft and connect the pipe to an air compressor, which you will wear, with the rechargeable battery, in a harness around your waist. The pipe when filled with air will stretch the earplug-like dick, lengthen it and fatten it until you are happy with it.'

Even though Chuck thought Doctor Dick was making too many references to earplugs, he had listened intently and responded, 'I don't really fancy that.' With his body giving a slight tremble, he added, 'That sounds a pretty painful method of dick enlargement to me, Doctor Dick. What's the other treatment you offer?'

Doctor Dick Bigg-Widdler said, 'My alternative and most popular method involves the removal of the earplug-sized dick and the grafting on of a baby elephant's trunk as its replacement. I will connect the tubes, veins, arteries and nerves. It will feel like and act in every way as a healthy dick. It will look very large hand held and ladies will find the dick extremely pleasing.'

13

'I will have to ask my girlfriend what she thinks of your second suggested dick treatment, Doctor Dick,' Chuck said, 'she's outside waiting. I will go and ask her now.'

When Doctor Dick Bigg-Widdler heard Betty's squeals of delight echoing from the waiting room, he knew he had succeeded in selling his treatment, his expertise. He immediately rang his travel agent to book a shooting safari in Africa's Kruger National Park, during the imminent elephant-culling season. Then he booked cryogenic storage and arranged for the safe shipment of the trunk to his clinic. Even baby elephants were a huge target. He was sure of a successful shoot.

The operation was successful. Chuck was delighted. Betty was more than satisfied with the result of the enlargement. They announced their engagement.

Chuck's future in-laws held a betrothal celebration dinner at their home. Chuck and Betty sat together at the dining room table. Hidden beneath the overlapping tablecloth, Betty's hand stroked the length of Chuck's, newly acquired, mammoth manhood, couldn't leave it alone.

Suddenly, the mammoth manhood burst through Chuck's boxers, shredded all the buttons from his trouser's fly, reached out and snatched a baked potato from a plate on the table, then disappeared beneath the table with it.

Several of the guests were temporarily gobsmacked, couldn't believe what they had just witnessed. Betty's mother screamed, 'What the fuck was that? I'd sure like to see that again.'

Chuck said, 'Well, I wouldn't. I don't have room for another potato up my arse!'

BLACKPOOL BOXING

That October morning, the Blackpool Forfree Club management thought they had covered every detail, every eventuality, for the entire female-only boxing show. The show included a Women's Heavyweight World Title event. That was special; would put the venue on the World Boxing Map. For the first time, the North West of England's world famous concert hall of entertainment and seaside refreshment was hosting the sport.

Management had finished the mounting of boxing paraphernalia. The venue now looked like an old time boxing booth. It would also smell like one. Tobacco smoke scented capsules in smoke generators, occasionally blasting out, would make the olde-worlde atmosphere authentic. Enlarged pictures of previous women world champions adorned its walls. The better-known and world-renowned female boxers on view included the Sioux Red Indian Pocahontas Canvasser, the Russian Ivana Knakkerov, the Thai transvestite Gregory Ladyboy, Irish heavyweight star Rosy Butt and the French legend Fanny Liqueurs.

The preparations were simple tasks for the town's experienced tradesmen. They had fitted thousands of light bulbs, prepared, repaired and devised new, complicated attractions for the greatest light show on Earth, 'The Blackpool Lights'.

Each holiday season, millions visited the seaside haunt. Travelling by tour bus or by other means of transport, from towns and villages north and south, they came mainly to see the lights. Humour lovers amongst them might deviate or linger to enjoy the entertainment promoted in the famous piers, theatres and bars. Comedians such as Roy Chubby Brown and the new booking to the resort, Billy Bagman, were big named acts. The more sedate could view the wax effigies of the famous and infamous in Madame Tussaud's museum. Arcades would fleece the unwary of their change in rigged slots. The adventurous would mount a donkey on the sands for a wonky ride. Many just drank themselves silly. Some visitors, bolder and adventurous, spent a long-weekend in one of the thousand or more guesthouses and hotels. Management had sold all of the boxing event's tickets; they were happy with their advertising and preparations.

The Forfree Club doors opened at 19:00 hours. The waiting queue filed into the venue. The bar servery stretched along the entire length of a wall. The dozen or more bar staff waiting behind it were eager to begin pouring the many weak beers for which Blackpool is famous.

Soon, attendees filled the available seating. A tuxedo dressed, muscular, butch looking female ring announcer, black string tie hanging from the shirt collar, mounted the stairs to the elevated ring. Carefully, she parted the top and middle ropes and stepped onto the canvas. She hissed into the microphone held in one white-gloved hand. Turning her head, she listened for an audible snake-like response through the venue loudspeakers.

The first match of the evening was of six rounds between two of Lancashire's lightweight women. The first girl to enter the ring was Goya Lovejoy from Preston. Her friends, family and fans knew her as Go Lo. She had a hungry, dogged, undernourished look about her. The mascara around her eyes made her look ghoulish and she had no breasts of note. Not many friends had treated her to tasty, filling meals in the city's many kebab takeaways and Indian restaurants. She had no arse to comment on hidden away in her baggy shorts, but sported a hairstyle fashioned to look like a hand-grenade. Greta was in the Blue corner.

Florence Floorwalker, known affectionately as Flo Flo, hailed from the City of Salford. Flo Flo towered over Lovejoy by a good six inches. She appeared to have had her ample breasts strapped down and enclosed in a protective, restraining apparatus, which her t-shirt didn't cover too well. Flo Flo trained in The Clowes gymnasium building, which once was a pub of ill repute, the haunt of locals, sailors, dockers and 'ladies of the night'. Situated outside Manchester's Dock gates, the pub was a very popular hostelry. Flo Flo was in the Red Corner.

The Salford girl won the bout in the first round. A well-directed uppercut to her opponent's undefended chin knocked her out. The Preston girl was taking some punishment when, foolishly, she enraged her taller opponent. She spat her gum shield out in Floorwalker's direction and shouted at her: 'You're nothing but a thieving, scummy, Manchester United supporting cow.'

There were six other bouts of varying weights, none as dramatic as the first, before the heavyweight contest for a World Championship title and belt.

There was much hurrahing for the heavyweight bout. Bonny Bottomly, the Scottish challenger from the island of Benbecula, known to her fans as Bo Bo, emerged from her changing room. She wore a saltire wrapped around her shoulders. A Celtic top covered her to protruding waistline. A kilted Black Watch piper, playing the poignant Dark Island tune, led her along the short passageway through the audience to ringside. Emotion effected several Scottish supporters seated in the front row. Tears spilled down their coupons already reddening with excitement and the fortification Buckfast Tonic Wine the bar offered.

Showing her athletic dexterity, Bonny raced up the steps to the ring and somersaulted over the top rope, clearing it by a good six inches. Miraculously, she landed upright and on her feet. Scottish fans noisily cheered for a full minute. Then more cheering broke out. Bonny performed some fancy highland dancing footwork as the piper transitioned skilfully from Dark Island to the upbeat The Hen's March to the Midden, a tune normally performed on the violin by nimble fingered fiddlers with supple elbows.

World Champion Djimima Decker's burgeoning fan base knew her as Dee Dee. Her Wikipedia CV stated that, previously to her boxing career, she was a Lincolnshire sausage knotter living Scunthorpe. Dee Dee appeared at the door of her changing room, the cloud of fake white smoke enveloping her partly obscured the sparkler showers, but didn't dampen the thunder of firework bangers exploding in her vicinity. Everyone knew she was there. Stepping out from the smoke, the championship belt strapped to her waist glistened in the glare of the overhead lighting. Bustling along the short passageway to the ring, Dee Dee touched fans' hands reaching out to her. Scottish supporters were shouting raucously, 'Who put the cunt in Scunthorpe?'

Ignoring the insults and swinging her backside in contempt, Djimima leapt up the stairs to the ring. Bending, showing a fine crack, a vertical smile to die for, she slipped between the middle and top ropes. It quickly became apparent that Dee Dee's nose had been broken a few times and looked filleted.

The seconds gathered in their official corners. Preparing their charges for the ten rounds of boxing ahead, they applied Vaseline to eyebrows and gave last minute instructions and encouragement.

The ring announcer, her story about the relevant championship decider over, described the contestants: 'In the Blue Corner, we have the challenger, Bonny Bottomly, known in the Western Isles of Scotland as Bo Bo. She hails from the sleepy Island of Benbecula. This morning, Bonny weighed in at twenty stones eleven pounds. She is a worthy challenger, undefeated in forty contests. She is the present Highland and Islands heavyweight champion. She was this year's runner up in the Highland Games men's Caber Tossing final and qualifier in the men's How High Can You Piss Contest. This strong woman has easily lifted the four hundred and fourteen pound weight Dinnie Stone since she was fourteen years of age.

'In the Red Corner, we have Djimima Decker, the world champion. She is undefeated in fifty contests. She is this year's winner of Lincolnshire's Canal Vaulting, Worm Charming and Bog Snorkling championships. She is the five times winner of Scunthorpe's Arse of the Year. Djimima hails from that leafy town. This morning, Djimima weighed in at twenty-two stones thirteen pounds. The timekeeper for this bout is Ken Ticker-Bell. Your referee, all the way from Houston Texas, is Dick Dribble. Contestants, come out from your corners fighting and may the best woman win.'

The bell clanged for round one. The boxers touched gloves and faced off. In the first minute the boxers circled, each trying to command the centre of the ring. Gloves touched several times, fending off jabs. During the round, neither boxer struck a telling blow. Rounds 2 and 3 were almost identical. Each woman seemed wary of the other's reputation as a big hitter and didn't venture within range of the other's hook, haymaker, uppercut or jab. The audience was getting restless at the continuing inactivity. A Scot's voice hollered, 'Put the bone back in her nose, Bonny.'

Rounds 4 began with a bang. Decker rushed from her corner to greet Bottomly as she rose from her stool. Bottomly ducked and slid underneath Decker's flailing arms, turned sharply and threw a swinging punch to land on Decker's head. Decker shook her head, threw it back, turned and smiled evilly, as if she had felt nothing. The audience roared encouragement as she responded with a solid biff to the challenger's ear hole.

There was little to report during the remainder of the round. Rounds 5,6,7,8 and 9 were similar affairs, both women resorting to bodywork, each receiving warnings for hitting low. The retired boxing elite present thought that the three ringside judges could only have judged any of the rounds as drawn.

The bell clanged for the 10th and final round. Bottomly had to pull something out of the fire to snatch victory. At the very least, she had to connect with a telling blow that impressed the judges. A drawn match entitled the champion to keep the title. Decker could see the aggression in Bottomly. She kept her guard high, retreated, kept out of danger. The retention of the heavyweight championship was near.

Then, what a mess: Decker's periods started, flooded the canvas and her second threw in the towel.

DOWN ON THE FARM

Dairy farmer Ivor Fourteats had looked at his books: the farm wasn't making the money it had in the past; milk yields were similar, but income had dropped. He knew the oversupply of milk from factory farms and imports of dairy products from the European Union were keeping low the prices paid to the traditional farmer for milk.

With plenty of rich grazing, Ivor thought increasing herd numbers and, therefore, production, was his best-earning option. However, his faithful bull, that he relied on to do the business of keeping the herd headcount up had, earlier in the year, lost its passion for fertilisation and, with earnest cajoling, it had refused to mount a cow. Its life had ended as various cuts of butcher meat, mince, sausages and burgers.

Without a bull, there was no prospect whatsoever of homebred heifer calves being born and he feared some of his cows would soon cease lactating. To maintain lactation, his Friesian dairy cows must produce calves.

Raising cow numbers by producing heifer calves by artificial insemination was a reliable alternative to keeping a bull for the dairy farmer. However, with the bull of his choosing, Ivor knew he'd feel more confident of the calibre of the offspring born into his herd, and of their milk yield, once mature. Bull calves he had always sold on for veal; he needed new blood to breed the exceptional milking cattle he required to increase profitability.

Ivor needed a new, virile bull. He broached the subject with his wife, Janice, who was a still an attractive woman, much younger than he was; but closer to her mind was *her* lack of conjugal rights, not *his* cows'.

After he finished his assessment of how a new bull would increase herd numbers and milk production levels, she said to him, vociferously, 'You're keen to provide a bull with pleasurable experiences, but *you* cannot do the business with me, these days.' He had no answer to her jibe. Long hours and hard graft had taken its toll; his back ached constantly, was no longer as springy as a band saw blade and he'd no time for doctors.

Dryppen and Trype's Cattle Market was Ivor's nearest sales venue. They were holding a bull and cow sale the next day. The auctioneer's catalogue listed a number of suitable Friesian bulls for sale. He hoped he didn't have to bid too much for a young one, broad and sturdy with a cow-attentive attitude.

At the market, Ivor inspected the bulls in their pens. Sellers had smartly groomed most of the bulls on sale. Most had sought after pedigrees with testicles capable of improving his herd numbers with healthy stock.

In the ring, his £1500 bid secured Randy, an eighteen-month-old Friesian with a promising name and nice markings.

Ivor's first pangs of apprehension that he might have bought a dummy appeared when he first put Randy into the field with his cows. Randy had taken little interest in inspecting the cows, or sniffing about them for signs of oestrous. Instead, he was content munching at the field's succulent, clover-rich grass, and chewing away on it whilst looking distantly into the adjacent wood, his mind elsewhere, his eyes following the flights of pigeons.

Janice laughed at Ivor, shouted scornfully, 'He's not randy but gay.'

Henry Dryppen, the auctioneer who accepted Ivor's bid for Randy, was driving down a lane close to the farm two weeks after the sale. He stopped on spotting Ivor seated aboard a Kawasaki Mule, driving around a field, herding the cattle towards the farm steading. He hailed Ivor and waved him towards a gate. Ivor drove over, switched off the vehicle, dismounted and approached Henry.

Henry could see the worry lines besetting Ivor's face, when he enquired, 'How's Randy doing?'

'Total failure he is. He hasn't looked near a cow in two weeks. I put them into this field last week. It's lush with clover and I hoped it would make a difference, but no. He just wants to munch my pasture and silage and get fat. Look at him now. He's over at yonder fence and showing me his arse!'

'Oh deary me,' said Henry, 'I think you should see a vet and get something to gee the beast up. You cannot afford to be without a fertile bull, Ivor.'

The vet prescribed Ivor some tablets to force over the bull's throat. The transformation was instantaneous.

Two weeks later, Henry Dryppen was passing the farm again. He called in to speak with Ivor. When Ivor opened the farmhouse door, Henry saw a major change in his appearance. Gone were the worry lines, his eyes were bright, no blackish bags hung beneath them and he stood more erect. He asked, 'Tell me Ivor, have you been to the vet? I'd hate to have sold you an infertile beast'

'Sure I have, Henry. The vet gave me some tablets and I've dosed the bull with them. They've worked a treat. Not only has he served all my bulling cows, he's broken down fences to get to cows in neighbouring farm fields. Even the horses are bolting, quite wary of him when he sniffs them they are. I'm really pleased with his ability and stamina.'

'That's wonderful news, Ivor, but of interest and for future reference,' asked Henry, 'what's the name of these tablets?'

'I don't rightly know their name, but they taste like peppermints to me!' Ivor replied.

'Ivor, I'm out of the bath and about to warm the bed,' Henry heard Janice shout from atop the internal staircase.

'I'll have to go,' Ivor said, brightly, 'the wife spotted the difference the tablets made, too.'

BRUCE MEETS A GENIE

Bruce was strutting along Bondi Beach in his budgie smugglers. With his impressive gut hanging over the top, he had no chance of impressing the Sheilas sunbathing topless nearby with his stature. He wasn't getting any eye interest returned from the girls. They were completely ignoring him. Disconsolate at their lack of interest, when he saw the bottle lying partially covered in sand, he stopped, stooped and picked it up. Inspecting it, he thought the bottle looked ancient. The raised glass writing he could see said the bottle once contained 50-year old Bundaberg Rum. He was brushing off more sand to see if there was any more discernable writing when a genie appeared. With a glass in its outstretched hand, the genie said, in perfect English, 'Bruce, you have one wish. What will it be?'

Bruce exclaimed, 'Crikey, bloke, you took me by surprise. Now that you ask, I suppose I'd like to piss rum as good as what was in this bottle.'

With a click of his fingers the genie said, 'Bruce, you've got it. Whip out your donger smartish. Have a splash into this glass. Taste it neat. Let me know what you think.'

Bruce turned away from the girls. Being a modest man, he tugged his donger down the leg of his smugglers and had a splash into the glass. The colour looked flash. He raised the glass to his lips and had a taste. 'Fuck me, bloke, you're right about the rum. I'm glad I bumped into you. I was as dry s a nun's nasty. This Bundy is beaut, a regular bonzer drop. The best I've ever tasted, no fucking doubt about it. I'm gonna shoot through to the apartment now and tell my Marge. She likes a drop of rum, no kidding.

Entering the apartment in a breathless rush, Bruce saw Marge laid out on the lounge recliner. He grabbed her by the arm, pulled her to her feet and dragged her into the kitchen. He swilled out two glasses in the sink and dried them on a cloth. He dragged out his donger, stretched it and splashed a good measure into each glass. 'Here,' he said to Marge, stood looking on bemusedly, 'Take a sip of this nectar. It's the best fucking Bundy I've ever tasted. It's a ripper and 50-years old.'

Marge erupted, giving him a piece of her mind, 'Strewth, cobber. No way you're gonna get me to drink your piss! You must be off your fucking head, have a kangaroo loose in the top paddock. Who the fuck did you get that silly notion from. Did one of your drongo mates put you up to it? Did they, you dobber?'

'Naw, naw, Marge, you've got it all fucking wrong. I met a genie down at Bondi. He gave me one wish. This is it. I get to piss the best rum you've ever tasted.

Marge lifted the glass up to her lips. She took a tentative sip. Then erupted, totally gobsmacked, 'Gee, Bruce, you flash bastard, you're fucking right. The best Bundy I've ever tasted and I've sipped many. Bruce, you're as cool as a Fremantle doctor. Top up my glass.'

Bruce and Marge had a good night on the piss. I think that's where the saying comes from.

Next night, Bruce rushed home from Bondi. He headed straight to the kitchen. He picked up one glass, washed and dried it. Marge was close behind him. She shouted sharply and loudly, 'Where's my fucking glass you tight bastard?'

28

Bruce replied, 'Marge, darling, I'm gonna be generous. Tonight, you get to drink from the bottle!'

SEXY SPIDERS

From the backdoor step of the family home, a father was watching his ten-year old daughter, Angel, happily skipping in circles around the lawn. He smiled as he reflected that Angel had taken her beauty from her stunning mother, that she possessed the same sweetness, purity, love of the open air and nature. It was a warm, bright, sunlit summer's day. Birds fluttered around the feeders, tweeted in the trees and hedges lining the garden.

Suddenly, Angel stopped skipping to look intently at the ground. He walked over to see what work of God had captured her attention. He saw that Angel was looking at two spiders mating, watching the wonders of nature enfold.

'Daddy, what are those two spiders doing?' Angel asked.

My precious, 'The spiders are mating,' her father answered.

'What do you call the spider on top?' Angel asked.

'That spider is Daddy Longlegs,' her father answered.

'So, the spider underneath is a Mummy Longlegs?' Angel asked, seeking confirmation of her thoughts.

Her father's heart soared with the joy that his daughter had asked such an intelligent question. He knew that the sex education classes at school could have provided the answer, but he replied, 'No dearest. Both of the spiders are Daddy Longlegs.'

Angel, looking a little puzzled, lifted her head in thought, then raised her foot, stomped the spiders flat and said, 'Daddy, we're not having any of that Brokeback Mountain nonsense in our garden!'

THE VOLCANIC VINDALOO

Picture the scene: the dining area of an Indian restaurant. There's only two other customers, two men, sitting in a secluded corner, when a well-dressed woman enters. The woman chooses a table well away from the men. She removes the fur coat from her shoulders and places it on the back of the chair on which she chooses to sit. An Asian waiter arrives at the table, presents the woman with the leather bound menu.

'Would you like to order a drink?' the waiter asks the woman.

The woman said, 'Bring me a gin and tonic with plenty of ice and a slice of lemon, please.'

The woman peruses the menu. Her only other curry was a tepid, shop-bought packaged meal with little solid food content, but plenty of sweetening raisins. She did not like the meal. It is her intention to try a curry appreciably different. She is unaware her order of the volcanic tandoori chicken vindaloo is at the top of the chilli league of heat.

Sitting sedately at a table, the woman sips at her gin and tonic awaiting her meal to arrive. The same waiter appears pushing a trolley with a warm plate wrapped in a clean towel and two, stainless steel bowls on the top, along with cutlery and two complimentary papadums on a plate.

The woman takes few spoonfuls of rice from a bowl and builds a short stack on the warm plate. Placing the spoon in the curry bowl, she stirs the chicken around in the thick vindaloo gravy. She sniffs the curry before choosing two pieces of chicken, then two spoonfuls of gravy, which she places on top of the rice stack.

She contemplates, for a moment, how much chicken and gravy she should load onto her spoon: this is her first attempt at consuming an appreciably different curry.

She tentatively parts the larger chicken piece into two with the back of her spoon. Then she edges some rice grains and gravy onto the spoon, before popping her first vindaloo tasting into her mouth.

Almost immediately, she shoots to her feet, her face quickly turning the colour of beetroot. It appears that she cannot get her breath. She cannot expel the hot chilli chicken from her throat. She wobbles as she beats on her chest and begins to hyperventilate.

The two men sitting at a corner table are gay. They both look with concern towards the woman. Her breathing problems were signalling an imminent, physical collapse. They whisper to one another. Quickly onto their feet, they race across to the woman's table. Directly in front of the woman, the leading gay bends over and tugs his pants and underwear down to his ankles. His mate, close up behind him, sinks to his knees, extends his tongue, then inserts it between the cheeks of his partners arse, running it up and down in the crack.

The woman has led a sheltered life, had never witnessed such acts of unpleasantness. Reading in a woman's magazines about what some men do to each other had caused disgust. She sees the act portrayed in front of her as one of the utter depravities the magazine described. The woman convulses and the vindaloo chicken piece shoots from her mouth like an

Exocet missile, closely followed by a fiery trail of rice and ultra hot gravy.

The gays return to their table. The bender says to his mate, I told you the hind lick manoeuvre really works.

AN INVITATION TO THE GREAT AUSTRALIAN WANK OFF

Your prowess at many England All Comers Annual Wanking Contests has reached the Antipodes. Known universally as G.A.W.O, The Australian Grand Cultural Society for the expansion of Masturbation, and the organisers of the celebrated event, request your participation at next year's Great Australian Wank Off, on Waltzing Matilda Day, the date each year of the event.

This is an open-air event. This year it is taking place away out, beyond the black stump, alongside the now reputedly haunted billabong mentioned in Australia's flash, alternative National Anthem. It is a highly authentic venue: the original coolabah tree still stands, older, more gnarled and the lake still contains sweet, cool spring water.

Last year, our contest, on the banks of Moon River, nearest township Yorkies Knob, was a disaster: flies entering the supplied wanking lubricant disrupted wanker wrist action and concentrations.

We will not allow any jumbucks to stray into the competitive area. In previous years, this, too, has distracted attentiveness to the task. We bar ankle biters from entering the competition area. We do not wish to encourage blindness or palm hair growth to blight Australian youth. Organisers will provide Foster's Amber fluid, both draught and tinnies.

In recent years, the yardstick set by bonzer wankers, was their ability to fill a Billycan, normally a three Pinter, over the course of the three-day event. A banana bender Queensland bloke won last year's contest. He was whacking his donger and busily firing semen like bush oysters shooting down a cobber's rancid hooter; as industrious as a cat burying shit in soft loam. We describe these performances as a fair dinkum standard, which competitors will need to meet to stand a winning chance. As in previous years, there will be special prizes for individual performances.

The best performance ever seen on a world stage was at last year's England All Comers event. For the first time, a wanker achieved a quadruple ejaculation from a single hard on. This world record stands out like 'a shag on a rock'.

We would hope to see any contestant emulate this amazing feat during a performance at the prestigious down under event. If you do, we reckon the record will remain unbeaten for some time. Of course, a male, alien entity might land on Earth that has three cocks and premium-loaded testicles.

GAWO: THE RESULT

The Australian Grand Cultural Society for the expansion of Masturbation, allowed the immigrant, Helmut Gripper, his hometown the appropriately named Wank, in Southern Germany, to participate as sole European representative at this year's annual, Grand Australian Wank Off event.

Helmut won this year's contest by just a teaspoon of juice over contestant Rob Froth, who filled a three Pinter billycan almost to the brim, which was less than the winning jerk needed to overtake Helmut's pulsing effort, on Waltzing Matilda Day.

Helmut's likely participation had scared off Pommie wankers. In previous years, a trickle of pommes entered. Some of you even won the much sought after accolade. The board, ejaculate this response to you, 'Shame on you Pommes. You are a load of useless wankers.'

However, we had a record turnout at the fabled billabong. A photo finish decided the winner. Most contestants filled their billycans to a millimetre from the brim of their three pinter standard issue. This year's result might have thrown up a different result had judges been able to estimate just how much fluid wankers let dribble between their fingers during practice sessions.

The gentle resonance created by 10,000 rhythmic, flip-flopping bobby's helmets, intrigued visitors within earshot. Visitors viewing Uluru, a red stone sticking out of the desert some 500 miles north of the fabled billabong, experienced this far-travelled, unusual, throbbing occurrence. The Australian Tourist Board has quickly cottoned on to this phenomenon;

they will advertise that attendees at all major attractions will hear a recording of the sound and feel the throb in coming years.

Missing from the Aussie repertoire of natural sounds, since Pommes incarcerated one of our most masterful musicians, is the throbbing of the didgeridoo. Aussies love throbbing. Playing the sound and the creation of this fantasy pulsation will increase interest in the red stone and other Oz cultural magnets, and fire up visiting numbers during our annual event.

NEWSPAPER DELIVERY

A teenage paperboy was delivering papers to a high-rise block. At an apartment new to him, a stunning young woman opened the door. The young woman was wearing a robe that didn't cover her entire body, showed her ample bare breasts had erect nipples.

The paperboy stood gobsmacked, but he manages to say. 'Hello, here is your paper.' His eyes, drifting downwards, lock onto the revealing gap that has suddenly appeared in her robe. It becomes obvious to him that she is wearing nothing beneath......top or bottom! He quickly looked up, trying to make eye contact with her. He knew not what he should do or say next. He started sweating profusely, shaking a little.

Seeing the paperboy's confusion, the young woman placed her hand on his arm and said, 'Let's go indoors, I hear someone coming.'

The paperboy followed her, dumped the papers inside the hallway of the apartment and kicked the door closed with the heel of a foot.

The young woman turned, opened the belt on the robe, shrugged a shoulder, let robe fall and settle around her bare feet. Now nude, she purred at him, 'What would you say is my best feature?'

Flustered and embarrassed, the paperboy, in a voice that squeaked, said, 'It has to be your ears.'

Astounded, and a little hurt, the young woman asked, 'My ears? Look at these breasts; they are a full 38 inches and 100% natural. I work out every day and my buns are firm and solid. I have a 28-inch waist. Look at my skin. There's not a blemish anywhere.

How can you think that the best part of my body is my ears?'

Clearing his throat, the paperboy stammered... 'Outside, when you said you heard someone coming, that was me!'

OLD FIRM UPDATE

Update from the Parkhead area of the City of Glasgow. This is another unbiased report from our man on the ground, William Proddie, head reporter of The Govan Glory, the favoured rag of the Ibrox loyal.

Doom prophecies are the garbled talk on the lips of the Celtic faithful. Supporters fear the worst. Celtic's poor early season results and Ranger's classy new signings concerns them deeply. On every pavement, worry beads clack continuously in grubby hands. The local priest has opened the chapel door to allow the anxious prayer opportunities. The magic word 'teninarow' isn't working as well as the conjuror's abracadabra.

Celtic supporters, fearing Ranger's upsurge in form and results will snooker any hopes of Celtic achieving 'teninarow', see ahead a decade of glory for the Govan loyal. The burgeoning anxiety complex is leaking down and affecting an increasing number of Celtic's fringe fanatical faithful.

Plagues of wide-eyed, dishevelled, pale-skinned, incoherent, manky degenerates, many ginger-headed or balding, all peculiarly dressed in hooped tops of white and green and orange tracksuit bottoms, roam Gallowgate and Tollcross, seeking safe havens.

Proper hygiene is an increasing problem. Many cross-eyed individuals, smelly and unshaven, male and female, have taken to living in squalid conditions.

Warrens dug on the consecrated land of the Eastern Necropolis, as sanctuaries for families, crisscross ancient graves. Warren residents use fallen headstones for toilet facility construction and as covers for tunnel entries and exits. Fear-ravaged, poorly focused eyes, scanning the terrain at ground level, warn of intruders. Settlers form headstone circles and fight off determined squatters.

Extremely disaffected members of the 'Lennon-out-brigade' affected with the prevailing malignant despondency syndrome and too ashamed of Celtic's form to show their faces, gather in already overcrowded sewers. Piss, an increasing shit deluge, crumpled, brown-tinged redtop newspaper squares inhibits flow towards Daldowie water treatment plant.

In later editions, William Prodie will comment on anything he considers unusual taking place.

GOVAN GLORY ARTICLE

Rome: Sunday.

The Pope's Sunday performance was over and he felt knackered. Spouting words in Latin for an hour to his many followers, from a sunblitzed, south-facing Vatican window, had taken its toll of the eighty-five year old pontiff. Wearily, he trudged to his quarters to shower. Pausing in his toilet, he splashed a much-needed discharge into a urinal bowl, manufactured in Glasgow's East End by decorative vitreous-china makers, Lourdes, Lennon, Adams & McGuinness, Ltd. Embedded in the glaze, the mugshots of Protestant pastors Paisley, Jack and Knox glared out at the Pope, but were blurring quickly beneath his stuttering, yellowy drizzle.

He undressed in the privacy of his personal shower room. He fiddled with the taps and set both hot and cold to deliver the correct tepidness in the cubicle. His ancient skin blistered easily these days. Using a fragrant gel made by Buckfast Abbey monks skilled in soap making, and the distilling of an important, Glasgow-linked beverage, he lathered up. His crevices cleansed, he raised his cogliones (testiculis) and began to stretch out the wrinkled skin of his scrotum, comparing it briefly with that hanging from an elbow (cubitus).

Detecting a stiffness rising in his pene, the Pope grabbed it lest it quickly disappear. Toying gently, he brought his "old fella" (senex quis) to hardness, then continued to pump the holy meat (cebus sancti) briskly until nearing the vinegar stroke

43

(ictus aceto), when his feverish jerking slowed, prolonging the moment.

The Pope's legs wilting, his back arching, he waited the finality of the masturbation. The holy load was shooting into the near distance as he opened his eyes and, looking upwards, he saw a member of the dreaded paparazzi busily snapping-off photos of the event through a skylight window!

'Merda, arrestare, (shit, stop)' cried the Pope, 'what do you think you are doing here?'

'I'm taking photographs to sell to newspapers, Your Holiness.'

'How much will they pay you?'

'Two million Lira.'

'I will buy the camera and the pictures, how much?'

'Two Million Lira,'

'Merda doppio. (double shit)'

A little later, the Pope, dried and robed, was walking towards his quarters. He passed by Sister Maria Chastity who attempted to draw him into conversation. She asked him in her rough Belfast twang, 'Bayjasus, you've a neat wee camera there, Holy Father. How much were you diddled out of for that at the rialto?'

'Two million Lira.'

'To be sure, Your Holiness, did somebody see you coming?' she asked.

THE TRIAL OF AMOS MANDINGO

Judge Lucifer Goebbels said in sentencing. 'Amos Mandingo, you are a disgrace to your Ma and your Pa that dragged you up, your brothers and sisters, uncles and aunts, your cousin and best friend Andy, your neighbours in the ghetto, and the whole black community. I sentence you to a term of not less than twenty and not more than forty years in the state penitentiary.

'The jury of good, upstanding white folks have found you guilty of committing the horrific crime of multiple rapes. While confined, you will undergo a period of correction to curb your warped, sexual appetite. If normal psychiatric consultations fail to improve your demeanour and behaviour, I will authorise immediate, physical castration.'

You might guess from my name that I'm as black as the proverbial Earl of Hell's waistcoat. From those dreadful words of Judge Goebbels, I deserved the confinement he's given me. I feel I am just unlucky. If you're as unlucky in life as I feel I am, then you'd be staring at the same iron bars from the ceiling to the ground with graffiti all around. My large dong put me behind these bars. Whose fault is that, I ask you? I didn't ask to be born this way.

I reckoned the Judge had it in for me cos the prosecutor, in his introduction, kept on telling the jury I was well hung. About the same time as the prosecutor mentioned this indisputable fact, an uproar in the public gallery occurred. A fat old bitch of a white woman, with a flap mouth and a bustle thrusting out from her already fat ass, who'd followed the case from day one, because she'd heard talk of the introduction of a big dong in court, shouted. 'Judge, he should be bloody well hung.'

I'd been thinking all of my time in court that the Judge was a ladies man. He ogled on Mary Lou's titties at every opportunity, when she gave her evidence against me. And I'd heard it said he was a wizard beneath the sheets. Now, I reckon I's slightly wrong in believing that assumption one way and slightly right in the other. I can still see Judge Lucifer Goebbels, peering with a half-smile over his half-glasses. He enjoys what he's doing. And I hear those words barked from his klu klux clan soul, that rattled my senses so much, words that convinced me never to get another hard on. Currently, I reckon, he must have been an inch or two short of a reasonable length dong, he wasn't getting his oats and that's why he gives me the long sentence.

In the cell beneath the courthouse, the big black guy in the next cage must have heard about me too; he's been ogling me, whistling and winking, weighing me up and down. His eyes are leery. Grabbing his crutch, he says something about busting my black ass if we get to the same pen. Afraid, I ignore his interest and just sit, clenching my ass cheeks.

Well I know what's ahead of me now as I sit here, my back to a wall, my head in my hands, shackles tight around my ankles. My dong has taken flight and disappeared up its own canal. Soon the dreaded prison bus will transport me to the pen.

I knew I'd no chance of saving my scabby ass when I caught sight of the Counsel the state had given me. Dingus Dreadnought had the unhealthy facial features of an undertaker that told me he was soon going to die. He never asked me nothing, just said,

'Boy, you and me together we're going to get you out of this mess. I'll just tell the jury your story as it happened, and we'll throw you to the mercy of the court.'

Well, when I heard that I thought right away, this geezer's a fully paid up member of the clan, that's for sure. He wants to see me dancing on the end of a line as well.

I've been the butt of jokes over the length of my dong for a long time, ever since I was at pre-school. Hell, in short trousers it would hang out of one leg all of the time. When I grew up, it wasn't only the white guys that caused me continuous irritation. My lifelong friend and full cousin, Andy Mandingo, a man not half as blessed in the dong stakes, he's at it too. He started the ache in my groin that has sentenced me to suffer for a period of not less than twenty years in the pen.

He said to me at the height of last summer, when the hormones were pulsing through my veins for the first time, driven by the musty smell of babes sweating in the sun, the same sun kissing my back. 'Amos, you's 18 years old now, and if you's so well hung, why's you's not trying it on with that Mary Lou, her with the big titties and nice ass. The bitch is always ogling you. She must have seen your bulge, or you draining your prunes up behind the school bike shed or something.

Mary Lou, a nice Mulatto girl, lived down in the crinkly tin constructed houses. Cows ran wild there with shit spreading across the streets. She had a pretty round face, a pair of voluptuous lips, a generous mouth and ultra-white teeth. She had black, silky hair that flowed all the ways down her back to her beautiful, light-brown ass.

She'd always be with her Ma or her Granny walking together on the sidewalk. I could never get close to her, but as Andy said, she sure ogled me some. I never reckoned why cos really I's an ugly fucker when you boils it all down. A flat African nose with nostrils like the Manhattan rail tunnel, with plenty of room for the bone white dudes told me should be stuck in there. The hand grenade hairstyle I was born with was difficult to change in style.

Summer nights stayed hot in the small Mississippi township of Chubbsville. And the August night that Andy says to me, 'Amos, let's go around to Mary Lou's house around about her bedtime and sneak a look through her bedroom window,' was no exception.

'We can't do that,' I screams back at him, 'if us black boys gets caught they'll whip the nuts off us with a rusty knife, that's for sure.'

'But just think of those lovely titties, hot and sweaty, swinging about with no support, and her pussy getting some air before she jumps beneath the mosquito net into bed for the night.'

Well, his lurid descriptions surely hooked me, and I beat hell out of my meat for three consecutive nights. Ma was not amused. Next morning I could hear her thrashing around, wrestling and beating into shape stiff sheets as she remade my bed. She shouted so all could hear, 'That dirty big boy of mine has been masturbating again. God rest his soul.'

Something just had to give, and lured by Andy's lurid descriptions that he was at pains to repeat, I, stupidly, as I know now, went along with his devious plan.

On many, long summer evenings, Mary Lou and all the members of her family would sit for hours on the veranda. They'd listen to the call of the toads and the snap of alligator teeth coming from the swamp, the scurry of rats crossing the mud track and from beneath the house and the flitting of vampire bats attacking the braying family mule. They extended their entertainment chucking stones to frighten the bats away. The bats might be blind but they could always dodge the stones

Mary Lou's Granny sat in her rocking chair, smoking a pipe, with her pince-nez glasses perched on the end of her nose. She told family stories of the bygone days of slavery in a thin, croaky voice. She occasionally stood up, raised her loose cotton smock, and wafted much needed, cooling ventilation around her overheated backside. Mary Lou, along with her ma, little sisters and little brother, would sit and intently listen. When the granny had finished her tales, they'd have a feast, suck meat from the jawbones of boiled pig's heads, and polish off plates of fresh chitterlings. At 10 o'clock each night, Mary Lou's ma would signal with her thumb that it was time for bed. 'Though you don't need it, go and get your beauty sleep, my Mary Lou, honey,' was what her Ma would always say to her.

The night we done it, Andy and I, we waited until we see the signal and hear her ma say the magic words. We made our way around the back to Mary Lou's bedroom window. We did it quietly, the braying noises coming from the mule made it easy.

We gets there keeping low down, in shadows and hiding behind bushes.

It was as Andy said; Mary Lou's window was wide open and so was our eyes as she got her gear off. She pranced up and down in front of her mirror, titties nice and round, pointed, with pert nipples that curved upwards, as if she was dying to have someone watching her. Then she lay down on the bed, arches her back and moans as she fingers between her legs just where her pussy is. I didn't know rightly what she was doing to herself, but I sure got hard. And in a spasm that nearly broke my back, I shoot my stuff down my leg. I think Andy had done some too cos we both walked home oddly, jeans sticky on our legs, with wet patches appearing down to the knees.

I was sure she knew I was there cos next day, when she's walking a little adrift from her Ma, she says to me coyly, but with a big come on smile, 'Get a good eyeful last night Amos?'

Well I was shocked, but Andy said, 'that's the biggest come on I've ever heard, she sure after you to give her some pleasuring.' Well he's a good deal older than me so I believe him. That's how my troubles started.

My hormones started to run higher and my Ma was keeping a good eye on me. She was checking for movements coming from my bed throughout the hot, southern nights. I couldn't sleep, just tossed and turned. Definitely more tossing of the pleasant, flip-flopping of the old helmet style. I was knocking flies from the ceiling with a well-aimed globule of the shooting juices.

'I'm going to send them sheets to the church for the pastor to see, if I gets anymore of your foul habits soiling them,' ma threatens me.

Life was hell and there was me walking around all day with a root on like a large, hard bamboo stalk. And my nuts were painfully too. They stood out as if on the end of piano wire, for reasons not yet fully explained to me. Mary Lou didn't help. She knew she'd got me going. She'd begun to wear low-cut dresses that showed a good eyeful of tittie. I liked that, but it just made me harder.

The night I cracked and did the foolish deed, I remember well. My dong had been heavy and lugubrious all day. It had jerked compulsively and it took to rising fast without much thought from me. It was indicating its readiness for some serious, pleasuring action. My nuts were in some pain and when I pushed down on them, they'd spring back up, still attached to the piano wire of my imagination. Mary Lou had passed by me on the sidewalk, brushed against me, letting me have a whiff of the rich mixture of sweat she was generating and the expensive perfume her Ma had lashed on her. That sure engulfed me. It was a real turn on. I had chronic, unrelenting hardness and more pain in the nuts as a result.

After I'd done Mary Lou and her family, all with the same erection I may add, the hue and cry was louder than anyone could remember since the last slave run away from his plantation with the white owner's white wife. Andy hid me up in a barn under a pile of straw heaped with mule dung. But one of those confident black Labs, the ones with the pointy, wagging tails and the permanent know all smiles that's taught to sniff out anyone in soiled boxer shorts,

51

soon had me transfixed in its stare. The cops nicked me.

The Judge didn't look too pleased with me from the moment I entered the dock to hear the charges against me. Four counts of rape, attempted bestiality with a small dog that I strongly deny and damage to a pair of pince-nez glasses. There were groans from my Ma and Pa sitting at the back of the court and shouts of 'string him up' from some white dudes that kept on taking white hoods with eye slits from their pockets and doing trial fittings. While others shouted, 'How low can you get?' The answer was, that night, I'd have got as low as a Chihuahua, so randy had I become.

My Counsel, what a waste of space he was. Never put me on stand. Said it would be better if I said nothing. 'Keep your trap shut or you'll hang yourself boy,' he said.

Then he told the jury the state had no case against me. 'My client is a well-endowed young man who'd attracted the attention of Mary Lou, and her whole family showed interest in having him pleasuring them. Mary Lou, it appears to me, and from what my client has told me, was encouraged to flash her ample and very nice titties in my client's direction. This blatant act of enticement has led him on and to believe he was welcome to have sex with her. In so doing, he committed the acts as charged, and the court should release him immediately. Pleasuring is an act of pleasure, Your Honour. That's not a crime in my book.'

I'll give him his due; he tried to get Mary Lou to show her titties to the court. The Judge looked game, but the prosecution objected.

'Sustained,' said the Judge, disappointedly.

It was obvious nobody believed my Counsel's story, and the prosecutor, when he got his turn, went straight for the jugular, no messing.

'I call Mary Lou to the stand,' he said, with a knowing smirk in my direction.

Well, Mary Lou, she got on the stand and never looked at me once. All those sly looks, giggles and come ons were long gone.

The prosecuting counsellor said, 'Mary Lou, tell the court in your own words, what this here Amos done did to you and your family on the night in question.'

Mary Lou, she'd quite a high-pitched falsetto of a voice that increased in pitch as she went through her evidence.

'Well, it was like this Juuuudge. I'd never encouraged Amos. In fact, I never really liked him. He's an animal, Judge. His nose is too flat and his nostrils too big to attract the attention of a refined Mulatto girl the likes of me. And when he stormed onto our veranda that night, with his dong in his hand, it sure frightened me to hell. He dragged me from the floor where I was sitting, rips my knickers off in front of my Ma, my littler sisters, my little brother, the family dog, and my old Granny just sitting there in her rocking chair with her pince-nez glasses on smoking her pipe'

'Laudy, laudy. Mary Lou I've heard enough. I'm gonna send Amos to the pen for a long sentence.'

'But I aaiint finished yet Juuuuudge,' Mary Lou replied, in a shriller voice. 'Then Amos, he grabs my Ma and throws her to the ground, rips her knickers off and pleasures her in front of me. I'm weeping in the corner, getting protection from my littler sisters, my little brother, the family dog that's watching it all, and my Granny just sitting there in her rocking chair with her pince-nez glasses on smoking her pipe.'

'Laudy, laudy, roared the Judge,' his gavel banging up and down off his desk as he spoke. 'Mary Lou I've heard enough about this pervert Amos. I'm definitely gonna send him to the pen for a long, long sentence.'

'But I aaaiiint finished yet Juuuuuudge,' she said in an even shriller voice. 'Then he got hold of one my little sisters and tore her knickers off. Then he throws her to the ground with her legs flying in the air and pleasures her in front of my Ma, and me just sitting weeping in the corner, my little brother and the family dog watching. My Granny was just sitting in her rocking chair with her pince-nez glasses on smoking her pipe.'

'Laudy, laudy, laudy, laudy' said the Judge, banging his gavel down. He shouted, 'order in court,' at some unruly white dudes just dying to get their hands on me. 'Mary Lou I've just about heard all the evidence I need about this pervert Amos. I don't need to hear anymore. He's going away for a long sentence already.'

'But I aaaaiiiint finished yet Juuuuuuudge,' Mary Lou was beginning to screech, such was her vindictiveness, straining vocal chords in her effort to put me away.

The Judge, he's going mental, banging his gavel, shouting, "order in court," and directing an evil looking team of definite clansmen to leave the court.

'Then he got hold of my other littler sister, ripped her knickers off and back scuttled her over the veranda rail. He did it right in front of me and my Ma and one of my littler sisters. We all sat weeping in the corner Judge. My little brother and the family dog watched it all going on. My Granny, she just sat in her rocking chair with her pince-nez glasses on smoking a pipe."

'Laudy, laudy, laudy, laudy. I've heard enough, Mary Lou. Amos is going to go down for a long time. He might never see again the light of day. I don't want to hear no more about him.'

The court is in uproar and people who I thought were friends are shouting, 'hang him high.' Others shouted, 'get the castration knives and slit the nuts off this horny rapist.'

Then, when order is restored Mary Lou she starts again. 'But I aaaaaiiiiint finished yet Juuuuuuuudge,' she screams in a high, horrendous, demeaning, nut quaking, falsetto.

'Then Amos he goes for my little brother, but he's sharp and scurries away through a hole in the veranda. Then he goes for the dog that's been watching the goings on. The dog's having none of it, growls and follows my little brother down the hole. Then he turns to my Granny, and pulls her up from her rocking chair. She'd just sat there with her pince-nez glasses on, smoking her pipe. He throws my Granny to the ground, rips her knickers off with his teeth, and pleasures her with her pince-nez glasses still perched on the end of her nose, all in front of.......'

'Laudy, laudy, laudy, laudy, laudy' bawled the Judge. His face has turned puce and his voice is hoarse with hollering. He's going apeshit, waving his arms around, banging and wafting his papers all over the court.

'Have you quite finished Mary Lou?' he finally asks, 'so I can sentence this Amos and get him out of my court'

'But I aaaaaaaiiiiiiint finished yet Juuuuuuuuuuuuuuuuuuuuuuuuuuuuuudge.' Well, I'd never heard vocal chords sounding so stretched and strangled. She sure was giving it some venom. At that point, in Mary Lou's testimony, I was sure my asshole had just caved in.

'Then Amos takes hold of my Grannies pince-nez glasses, puts them on the end of his dong, and says. "Look round son, make sure you aint missed anyone."'

THE PUB PICK UP

That Monday, I had just arrived in the town as a construction worker. I was helping to build a chemical factory that would provide locals with secure, long-term employment, when we had completed the construction and disappeared to work elsewhere. Many of the blokes I met on site had been working there since the laying of the foundations.

During the morning tea break, of my first day on site, I enquired from my table companions if the town had any nightlife of note and of any pubs that offered entertainment and live music. It seemed to me that the older blokes weren't into pub-crawling, but the younger seemed to have an encyclopaedic knowledge of the town's drinking dens. My new workmates told me that the grab a granny night at the Golden Oriole pub was the town's main attraction on a Monday night and none of them would miss going. Apparently, the women were easy, man hungry, all looking for a drink and to shag any of the well-paid contractors working in town.

My digs were near the town centre. Two of my morning tea break companions, Tom and Harry, shared the same accommodation. The landlady only offered bed and breakfast so we ate fish and chips from the traditional newspaper wrapping before we headed to our rooms.

The weather was benign. After shaving, taking a shower and lashing on the aftershave, I dressed casual. I waited for my new companions in the sitting room lodgers had at their disposal in the digs. I was pleased to see Tom and Harry had dressed likewise.

We had a few pints in nearby pubs before we walked the length of the high street to the Golden Oriole. Grab a granny lovers crammed into the bar. The DJ played a mixture of music as we queued at the busy servery for an order. Finding a seat was out of the question; women of all the descriptions listed in God's catalogue of femininity had claimed the seats. The choice was unbelievable. Tom, Harry and I were definitely going to click, my thoughts. They both pointed out certs to me. They were looking for a fresh conquest.

It didn't take long for a woman to rub shoulders with me as I stood with a pint in hand. She was probably a regular and wanted to try out the new talent. I smiled at her, even though there were probably better lookers on offer who carried a bit less weight on their backsides.

She asked, 'You're new here?'

'Aye, I said.'

'You a Jock?' she asked.

'Aye,' I replied.

'I'm Gloria. Let's dance,' she said, grabbed an arm and pulled me to a table where I could put my pint pot down.

I was on the crowded floor with Gloria for a full ten minutes. She was all over me, kissing, her warm breath in an ear, thrusting her crutch into me, her hand slipping down between us to squeeze my stiffness.

Gloria was clearly rampant for sex. She took my hand and pulled me off the dance floor. 'I'm going to get me coat,' she said, 'then I'm going to take you home and fuck you.'

What was happening to me was the opposite of a grab a granny and Gloria only looked about twenty-five.

There was a taxi rank on the opposite side of the street to the pub. Gloria hurriedly dragged me there through the slow moving traffic. In the taxi, Gloria gave the driver an address in what I later learned was a side street about a mile distant.

Gloria lived alone, in a bedsit. It was tidy, but her bed was a single. We stripped and through our clothes onto the floor. In bed, there was no time for foreplay. I mounted her; we were both desperate for it. I gave her a good rooting, then fell asleep on top of her.

I've no recollection of how long I was flakers before Gloria woke me. When she did, she pushed me off; I landed on the opposite side of the bed to what I had clambered. There wasn't much room for both of us to get a good night's kip.

I drifted off, but later, in need of a piss, I got out of bed. I put feet on the floor, stepped forward in the dark, a foot dipping and descending into Gloria's sizeable china pisspot, filled to the brim with piss, shit, sheets of torn newspaper and knotted condoms. The pot, with my foot still inside, rocketed backwards. The contents sprayed everywhere, over the carpet, her in bed and me. The pot shattered against a bedpost. A razor-edged shard lacerated my skin from calf to ankle and sliced through my Achilles' tendon. I overbalanced. I shot forward, covered in shit. Hopping on one leg, I crumbled and fell headlong through the glass of a low window. I fell two metres onto a verminous tramp, lying asleep on the pavement. On the way down, I caught my bollocks on a railing spike, broke a leg, an arm and lost an eye.

I said to the patrolling constable when he came along, 'I'm sorry the tramp died as result of my accident, constable. In footballing terms, pundits have said that you're at your most vulnerable when you've just scored. From my experience, I'm quite sure that pundits definitely know what they are talking about.'

CUPID STUNT

Malky said to his dad, 'Dad, when did you first fall in love?'

'Well,' dad said, 'I used to go out drinking a lot when I was younger. I was always on lookout for an attractive girl to court. It took me a few years, then a drop dead gorgeous blonde girl started coming to the same pub. Cupid fired his arrow the first time I laid eyes on her, I can tell you. I was besotted.'

Dad went quiet. Then Malky said, 'Come on then, finish the story. It's interesting. What happened next?'

'Nothing,' replied dad. Just my luck, the wee prick missed and the arrow hit your mum!'

STAFF REDUNDANCY

The prevailing business conditions hastened the office boss to make the decision to reduce staff numbers. Profitability for the company was important. Even so, he did not relish telling Valerie or Jack, the last staff he had employed, that a redundancy was the only answer he could foresee. He would emphasise to them that, in fairness to his other staff, and by rights, last in, first out, one of them would have to go.

The office boss thought of himself as a fair-minded man. He didn't want to just arbitrarily toss a coin and decide who should get their cards. He puzzled over how he might decide, but it seemed a lottery was, after all, the best way to make the decision.

He eventually chose this solution. The first of the pair to enter the office on Monday morning and use the iced water machine, sited close to the office door, he would inform them of their job loss, and explain the redundancy package available.

Monday morning he entered the office early and sat watching the door to make sure he got the first arrival correct. The last thing he wanted was a photo finish. He hoped they did not arrive hand in hand.

Valerie entered first. She had been partying all weekend and had a debilitating hangover. She made straight for the iced water machine to take an aspirin. The boss approached Valerie and said, quite abruptly, 'I have to lay you or Jack off.'

'For fuck sake, Jack off,' said Valerie, 'I feel like shit this morning!'

CONFESSION

Geordie was on his deathbed. Horrible stomach pains had ravaged his health. Doctors couldn't diagnose what was wrong with him and had told his wife Netty the grim news: expect the worst.

Netty had been at Geordie's hospital bedside all night, but had snoozed in the uncomfortable armchair. She was quite awake when Geordie cried out her name.

'I have a confession to make,' Geordie said in a squeaky voice, 'I want to get it off my chest before I go.'

'Shush, darling,' Netty said, 'we've been together for fifty-four years. I know all there is to know about you.'

'No, I must die in piece. I must confess. I'll tell you everything. I've shagged your sister and your best friend. I've shagged your best friend's best friend. I've shagged your sister's best friend. I've shagged our neighbour's wife. I've shagged the bank manager's wife. That's why I couldn't get a mortgage from them. I've shagged the local copper's wife. That's why he did me for speeding when I was only doing 25 in the 30-mile an hour limit. I've shagged the milkman's wife and that makes a change and I've shagged your mother.'

Netty moved closer to Geordie to whisper in his ear. 'I know what you've done. That's why I've poisoned you, you bastard!'

STRICTLY COME FARTING

Radio Trumping announces their first crossover tournament in the Strictly Come Farting series. Such contests are popular in counties where horny goat weed, refried beans, fried onions and cheese crisps are the favoured dietary additives proven to produce a winning performance.

As the event title suggests, it requires the entrant to produce two bodily discharges; namely, to simultaneously ejaculate semen and vent anal gas. The timing between emissions is crucial; the shorter time difference between the two releases denotes the winner.

We are looking for competitors whose diet contains masses of legumes and onions. We expect all entrants will already have a propensity for producing classy masturbation techniques. With the aplomb gained from glorious achievements in strictly come farting contests worldwide, many will enter this event with assuredness, confident that, once again, they can timely expel their issues in our version of this unique challenge.

Timekeepers from Switzerland, astute at timing using a stopwatch in each hand, will adjudicate in this event.

REAR OF THE YEAR IN OZ

We welcome your nomination as a participant in the influential, but often maligned, Australia-wide contest "Rear of the Year". The Bute Prospector, the Cockatoo Guardian and the Cudlee Creek Advertiser report joyously of relevant comments reaching their poofter letters pages.

In recent contests, Adelaide's representatives have landed the bottom of the pile spot. Your peach-like derrière has obviously been spotted as desirable and free from zits as you masquerade in disreputable dunnies and found worthy of the nomination.

This year's contest venue must be home ground to you: the Dead Man's Pass Reserve.

Judges are experienced and practicing colonic irrigationists from the Tranquil Sphincter rehabilitation centre, Brisbane: Dunny. A. Commode, Alix. A. Butt and Fanny. R. Wishing. These past winners, banana bender Queenslanders, will judge the contest fairly.

THE SPANISH HOLIDAY

Jock and Margo had flown from Dice into Malaga airport to holiday on Spain's Costa del Sol each summer for many years. Jock loved the views to the glistening sea from his favourite golf courses there. He could always rely on the lushness of the course fairways he strode along, admiring the landscaping. He marvelled at exquisiteness of the greens, and fretted over the difficult bunkers. The bunker just across a lake, between it and the green, he found particularly treacherous.

Margo just loved to sunbathe in her bikini on the playas of the Mediterranean, and sample the variety of tasty tapas and Tempranillo wines beachside cafes and bars offered.

Jock had always found a willing partner at the course: a partner who could speak a bit of English and didn't cheat, to play a round with him. This year, the 19th hole was devoid of customers and no one lurked on the practice range to improve their driving, when he pulled up in the rental car. Peeved that he couldn't find a partner, he sought out the course professional.

The professional welcomed Jock back. Quickly he explained that the committee had increased course fees astronomically, resulting in a reduced membership and fewer holidaymakers using the course. However, the committee, in their wisdom, had introduced robots to partner players who, otherwise, had to play the holes solo. The professional informed Jock that the robot would caddy, take a shot alongside him, improve his swing and suggest tactics and the clubs to use on every hole.

Jock saw no alternative but to accept the offer. The robot had a better round than he did over the first 16 holes played. Jock thought the robots advice and tutelage was so good that he booked the robot daily for the entire fortnight's holiday.

The robot tutored Jock so well that on the final round of the holiday he equalled the course record.

Jock was ecstatic with that performance, but his game lapsed somewhat during the following, long, wet and cold Scottish winter.

The following year, Jock was glad to return to the Costa del Sol. He needed to feel the sun on his back, play golf, take the option of a robot, get his mojo back and return home again equally as proficient at the ancient game as he was the previous year.

At the course, Jock didn't bother to look for a human partner. He walked straight to the golf professional's office to hire a robot for the fortnight. Jock was dumbfounded to hear from the professional that robots were no longer available. The committee had decided to cease offering them as partners to players.

'Mercy me. Why, oh why?' Jock asked in an anguished voice, 'They were so good with club choice, knew the intricacies of every green. They were so instructive and very difficult to beat.'

The professional explained that local golfers, the bread and butter membership the course relied on in winter, complained so much about the Mediterranean sunshine reflecting off the robot's shiny metallic body, blinding them and interfering with their play that the committee decided to discontinue hiring robots.

Jock asked, 'Couldn't you have painted the robots with something nice like the Black Watch tartan to stop the reflection?'

The professional said, 'Oh we did exactly that, but the skirl of bagpipe that the robots kicked out was driving the locals crazy!'

GOLFING TRAGEDY

Howard and his wife Debbie had played many golf courses together, shunning opportunities to play foursomes with other couples. They both had retired early and played most weekdays when it wasn't raining. They both enjoyed the windups and the banter between them, when one had missed an easy putt, landed in a bunker or sliced a ball off the fairway and losing it. Sometimes the banter had led to a mock fight between them, but they always laughed it off, kissing and hugging in the end.

Following an early morning game, Howard staggered into the Accident and Emergency unit of the local hospital suffering a concussion, multiple bruises, two black eyes, with a five iron wrapped tightly around his neck.

The Doctor, quite shocked on seeing Howard's predicament, said to him, 'I've sent for the blacksmith to removed the iron from around your neck, but please, tell me how this happened to you?'

Howard said, 'Well, I was having a quiet round of golf with my wife, Debbie. At a difficult hole, I kidded Debbie that she couldn't make the green in one. Debbie said she could make it easily and didn't take a lot of care with her stroke. She sliced her ball into the adjacent cow pasture. We fell about laughing. I laughed so much that I fluffed my shot and my ball landed in the pasture.

'We both clambered over a stile into the field to look for them. I thought it a difficult search. There were a few cows munching away and the grass was long. There were thistles and cowpats everywhere. While I was looking around, I noticed one of the cows had something round and white at its rear end, beneath its tail. I crept up to the cow's backend quietly and lifted its tail. Sure enough, there, in front of my eyes, stuck right in the middle of the cow's behind, was a golf ball. On closer inspection, I saw it had my wife's monogram on it. Still holding the cow's tail up, I yelled to my wife, ''Hey, this looks like yours!''

I don't remember much after that!'

CADDY SHACK

Larry had not intended to play golf during his holiday, whilst staying in Killarney, County Kerry. He played the American professional golf circuit for a living and needed a break to wind down. Larry had walked around the edges of Lough Leane, taken the Ring of Kerry Scenic Drive and already he felt refreshed, so much so, he rebuffed the suggestion of fellow hotel guests that he should not depart without attempting the 200km Kerry Walking Trail.

A Killarney golf course was a short walk from the hotel. He had passed by a few of the holes on his walks and found the course interesting. Some of the fairways were steep, leading to the side of a hill. Many water hazards, small lakes and streams, suggested that only a professional golfer, like he was, would feel confident enough to drive every ball across them to reach a green.

Larry decided one round wouldn't harm his recovery from stress. He walked to the course, introduced himself to the professional, hired clubs, a buggy and secured the services of caddy Patrick Murphy. Larry asked the caddie if he would take a stroke alongside him, make a game of it.

Patrick agreed and beat the professional easily over the eight holes Larry had booked to play. Although Larry was peeved with his performance, he thought the caddie lucky, and said, 'Tomorrow, Patrick, if you caddy for me, I'll give you 100 Euros if you beat me again. What time do you want to play?'

Patrick agreed, and said, 'Ten o'clock, but I might be half an hour late.'

Next morning, Patrick arrived at ten and proceeded to beat the professional again.

Larry was feeling a bit peeved that a caddy could beat him twice, even though his swing was there and his putting ability was as good as ever it was. 'Okay,' he said, 'I want to play you again tomorrow, double or quits. I don't believe you can keep this run of luck going.'

Patrick agreed and said, 'To be sure, I'll be here for ten o'clock, but I might just be half an hour late.

Patrick arrived the following morning at 10. He played 18 holes and beat the Larry again.

Larry asked, as he handed over 200 Euros, 'Yesterday, you played the round against me left handed; today, you played every hole right handed. Why is that?'

Patrick replied, 'When I awake of a morning and the wife is laid on her left side, I play left-handed that day. If she's laid on her right in the morning when I awake, I play right-handed that day.'

Larry asked, 'What happens if your wife is laid on her back when you wake up?

'Well, that's why I'd be a half hour late,' Patrick said.

A VACUUM SALESMAN CALLS

Members of the vacuum cleaner sales team had given Harry the nicknamed Flash. Harry didn't mind the sobriquet at all, it only inspired him to continue achieving sales away beyond what any member of the team delivered for the company. True, he dressed flashy; the commission he earned placed him in an earning bracket that afforded that possibility. The suit he wore when out knocking doors Savile Row tailors had stitched together. He hadn't purchased it there, but found it on a hanger hanging on a church charity market stall, possibly donated to the charity by a widow not realising the suit's worth. He bought it for a £1 and it fitted him without major alteration and, indeed, it made him look suave. On the doorstep, and to others in the team, he looked the real deal.

The managing director called him into the office one day and congratulated him on his successes. However, the M.D had learned that dissention was rife amongst other members of the sales team, many threatening to resign because, they believed, the company was giving Harry the posh, prime sales locations and they the council estates inhabited by poorer, less likely to buy, customers.

I am allocating you the prime Lake District location, the M.D told Harry. I want you to visit farms there and convince farmers of the effectiveness and efficiency of our Whirlwind vacuum. The machine is too large and powerful for the urban housewife's needs. Explain to farmers how efficient this product would be at removing many of the farm detritus they carried indoors. I'm sure farmer's wives would be ecstatic at the possibility of keeping the farmhouse cleaner with the whirlwind in hand.

Being a country boy, Harry knew that some farmers were tremendously parsimonious; wouldn't part with the reek of their dung unless it was for money, his old granny used to say, whilst nodding her head sagely. He suspected this was the case when the farmer answered the door at his very first farmhouse call. The farmer looked dour, thin of face with beady eyes. He was wearing a khaki Army greatcoat covered in chaff, dung and dirt.

He handed the farmer the product pamphlets, pointing out the Whirlwind as the machine most suitable for a farmhouse, its amazing suction and easy clean bag system.

The farmer listened intently to Harry's spiel and then said, 'I will tell you a story. If you can answer the question it poses, I will buy my wife the Whirlwind vacuum cleaner.

'Yesterday, I was in the byre to begin that afternoon's milking by hand. We only have two cows. Milking the first cow went to plan as I knew it would. However, the cow I'd just bought from market turned out a taciturn beast. I'd just placed my pale beneath her udders and squeezed a teet when she kicked out at me. I found some rope and tied that leg up to a beam. Back in milking position, and just about to squeeze a teet, she kicked out at me with the other hoof. I'd plenty of rope so I tied that leg up to the beam. Back in milking mode again, she swished her tail at me. I feared she might take an eye out. I'd no alternative but to tie the tail to one side, out of the way.

'Before I settled back into milking position, I felt the urgent need to urinate or I'd wet myself. The old prostrate isn't functioning as it used to. I had my cock out when the wife walked into the byre. If you can persuade my wife I desperately needed a piss, I will buy your bloody Whirlwind vacuum cleaner.

50 SHADES O' FOOKIN' GREY IN GEORDIELAND

Part 1

Wae ma mate Lisa, a' wuz reet up tae the entrance o' the dimly lit doorway an' a read tha sign above our heeds that said CLAPPY VALLEY NIGHT CLUB. What kind o' fookin' place wuz this, ah wuz thinkin'?

We got intae tha smoky hellhole, then pushed through tha thick crowd. Twuz then ah saw him, a hinny propped up against the bar, a beautiful pot belly owerhangin' his Jeans, his complexion greasy, his hair lanky an he wuz smoking a woodbine, like ma da would, coughin' his guts oot. He wuz the yun fer me areet.

A got reet close tae him, pushed in and felt fer his bollocks. Wae them nestling in ma han' ah gave them a wee squeeze that hud him wincin'. Ah said tae him, 'Gan tae buy me a drink, yer fuckin' great, Geordie, wastrel bastard that ye are?'

He looked up, burped Noocastle broon in ma face, and said, 'Whae the fuck dae yer think yer speakin' tae, slag?

Me knickers were soundin' like a creamery in foo production by noo, moist, nae soakin' fookin' wet and a couldnae find the netty. A noo it wud be crackin' later.

Part 2

We started takkin'. Ee, we hud a lot in common. He wuz on the buroo and say wuz ah. 'Hoos it gannin?' he asked, his een a wee bit crossed. 'Takkin' me hame lass?' he mumbled.

But a kood tell he wusnae shy. By noo, he hud swallaid 8 pints o' Noocastle broon ale, am share.

Mind yeh, ah hud just knocked back fower advocarts.

'The fettle's fine an that's great, ye big, hinny bastard,' ah said, 'am nae a slapper, yeh ken, but yee'll haetae gee me a makkem-like shaggin' fer am stannin' here wae ma pants ringin'. You'll hae tae gee us a hand' tae ring them oot afore yeh get mounted like a pit pony on me.'

Part 3

We got tae ma counsel flat doon Benwell by taxi, but the twat had nae dosh so ah hud tae fookin' pay.

He kicked his feet oot o' his trainers and ee, what a fooking' reek o' cheese, rotten gorganzola, am share. An' a niver saw the trainer fleein' through the air an' shatter the glass on ma only decent bit o' furniture, ma chinee cabinet. An' his socks were foo o' holes. He wuz mingin', bastard that he wuz, but he wuz mine fur the night.

Part 4

He sat himsel' doon on my best deck cheer, the yin ah nicked fae the beach at Whitley cos a needed summit tae sit on. He called tae me 'Ower here.'

'Ma names nae Ower, ye drunkin raj, its Doris,' ah fookin' telt him. 'yer takkin' shite.'

But ah went an' sat on his knee. He run his hans' up my back, up past an' ower ma hump. Ah hoped he didnae mind it cos it wud cos him instafookinabilty when he went tae lay me doon on

77

the flair fer a shag. He undid the zip on ma parka. It fell tae the flair. ah slid ma fingers up under his T shirt, then a ripped it aff, all o' a sudden, like.

His Robert Rae designer jeans were a bit harder to take aff as ma false nashers couldnae get tae grips with the belt buckle. Then we baeth fell tae the flair.....

We fell to the flair in a warm togetherness. My Alsatian bitch had just shit a' ower the linoleum when a' wuz oot.

FIFTY SHADES OF SMOKE IN DUMFRIES

It is some town, this Dumfries. I'd heard it has a quaint reputation this Queen of the south, the babes here easy. Following the match at Palmerston Park on Saturday, it was my intention to stay overnight and go on the piss. It was long ways back to Brechin; away up in that much fairer county of Angus. With a few train changes on the way, I was unlikely to get home the same day, staying overnight made sense.

I got chatting to a woman sitting perched on a bar stool in a pub I sauntered into down by the river. Now I'm not saying the woman was overly big or obese, but she looked as if she might need a hammock to hump around her flaps. I said to her quite casually, as you might get away with this line of patter in a strange town, hoping for the best, 'Do you suck cock?'

She came back at me immediately, her eyes locking on to mine, 'It's never entered my head you smart bastard.'

I don't know how much drink was swilling about in her guts, but she began looking at me longingly, giving me the eye. When her eyes crossed, and began to wander in her head, it looked as if she had more eyes than a sack of seed potatoes. I could tell immediately that she did suck cock and wanted to get those voluptuous lips around my bell end, maybe in a sixty-nine; ruby lips so practiced that she'd sucked enough cocks to put a handrail round the Great Wall of China.

She dismounted the stool and stood close to me, rubbing her great tits up and down my chin. 'Buying me a drink, big boy?' She asked.

I was in.

Of course,' I said, with a bit of a stammer.

'Double Pernod with a Vimto chaser,' she said to the lurking barman.

It was at that precise moment I felt her hand playfully groping for my tackle, find my bollocks then give them a tender squeeze.

I was in.

She pulled a packet of Camel smokes from her jeans hip pocket, shook the packet until a ciggy poked its head out, snapped her lips over it and then lit it with a Zippo. She inhaled deeply and blew the smoke out, completely blanketing my head.

She put an arm around me and roughly pulled me to her. I felt her hot breath blowing into my ear, then her hot, moist tongue probing deep into my aural cavity. Then she planted her lips onto mine and I nearly gagged as her wax-flavoured tongue probed my epiglottis and attempted a wrestle with my tonsils.

I'd a hard on by this time.

I was in.

To ascertain just how far this woman might want to go, I asked her, 'How would you like me to carefully insert my rampant bell end into your smoky little orifice?'

'No way you're going to shag my arse,' she said.

I was out.

SUN WORSHIP DANGERS

Cynthia was a sun worshipper. She never went topless on any of the playas close to her Benalmadena Costa holiday apartment. But she had views to the Mediterranean and the Avenida Del Sol, which runs along the coast to join the Autovia Del Mediterraneo further west. Instead, she preferred to take a daily walk up to the flat roof of the apartment block and laze next to the small pool on one of the chaise lounges provided by the management. Although she could see the sea from the roof, that was close enough for her. The plastic waste and other unmentionables the waves swept onto the sand had put her off taking a dip in the Med.

Naked and relaxing on the lounger on a July morning, Cynthia fell asleep as the sun soared towards its zenith. She had arrived at her holiday apartment having endured a sleepless, stressful, delayed, overnight flight. She was in a bit of a tizzy when the racket started. The noise of sirens blaring, bells clanging that the emergency vehicles were making passing the apartment block had awakened her. She was sure there were ambulances, police cars and fire engines, and probably more than one of each vehicle in the convoy racing towards an emergency. She thought it must be a serious incident and decided to take a look and spot if they were heading somewhere local.

Cynthia rose from the chaise lounge and walked unsteadily, still half asleep, towards the building edge. The sun was glinting off the sea, affecting her eyes and her ability to judge distances. A flip flop adorned foot hit the small wall surrounding the roof and she overbalanced. Lurching forward, she fell over the wall and tumbled from the roof.

Fortunately, for her, the building was under repair. Contractors had erected scaffolding. Ex-pat tradesmen toiled on each level. On the topmost level, Cynthia fell into the arms of a bricklayer busily pointing the gaps erosion had left between bricks. 'Wow,' the bricklayer erupted as his trowel went flying. He was shocked at Cynthia's arrival into his outstretched arms. His shock quickly disappearing, he said loudly, 'What a lovely beaver. I'd love to wash my face in that.'

'Despicable man,' Cynthia hollered, 'put me down, you beast.'

Unhappy with the title, the bricklayer dropped her down through a hole in the walkway of the level.

The carpenter working on the level beneath was equally shocked at Cynthia's arrival into his outstretched arms. The hammer and chisel he was using to remove rotting timber from a window surround went flying. His shock disappearing fast, he erupted, 'What a lovely pair of tits you have. I'd truly like to titillate your nipples with the end of my tongue.'

Cynthia was having none of it and hollered, 'Put me down, you horrible man.'

Like his fellow tradesman, working on the floor above, he too dropped Cynthia through a hole in the level walkway.

Fifty feet from the ground and likely a certain death, Cynthia fell into the outstretched arms of the similarly shocked hod carrier, delivering cement to bricklayers working above.

Cynthia, fearing her luck had finally run out, screamed at the hod carrier, 'Suck my nipples. Kiss my beaver. Make love to me all night. Fuck me up the arse if you want.'

'Fucking slut,' said the hod carrier and threw her over the safety barrier surrounding the level, to the ground.

ANIMAL FARM

My daily paper today reports that Malaysian health officials have discovered traces of pig DNA in a British brand of chocolates on sale in Kuala Lumpur sweetie shops. Last year, the paper reported on worrying findings that some supermarket-packaged meals contained traces of horse.

I was worried away back in 1959 that some foods contained horse, when OXO won that year's Aintree Grand National.

A man was deep in an Irish wood whilst taking a shortcut along a well-worn path between two pubs. He found, lying on the path, a suitcase containing a fox and four cubs. Concerned, he pulled his mobile from a pocket, saw he had a connection, obtained the phone number of the local Prevention of cruelty to Animals office, and proceeded to telephone them.

The man explained the situation to the young woman telephonist answering the phone. The woman responded disgustedly at the fox's situation and said to the man, 'Oh, how awful, that's terrible,' then she asked, 'were they moving?'

The man replied, 'I don't rightly know, to be honest, but I think that explains the need for a suitcase.'

My mate rang me and said, 'Listen to this. You'll never believe what I'm going to tell you. Without a doubt, it's the bargain of the century. I've just bought a donkey jacket from a clothing stall down the market. The original price was £20, but I got it for £2 in the sale. It's supposed to be slightly imperfect, but I've inspected it carefully and the only thing I can find wrong with it is one of the sleeves is slightly longer than the other two!'

I was walking down the High Street with my girlfriend when we saw a dog performing contortions as it licked its bollocks. She looked at me coyly and whispered, 'I'd love to do that.'
I said, 'Watch it doesn't bite you.'

You can tell I was having problems with the bird. I telephoned a bird assistance organisation. I must have dialled the wrong number. They said unless she had shit on my roof and my gutters were blocked they couldn't help.

A Red Indian introduced me to his girlfriend. He said, 'This is four horses.'
I said, "Wow, what a beautiful name, does it have a meaning?'
He said, 'Nag,nag,nag,nag.'

Govan Glory Report: Glasgow Police get a bum steer. Reports that Neil Lennon was thieving from Parkhead have proven to be untrue. He was only leaving the stadium with an old wooden railway sleeper over his shoulder.
Apparently, he was taking some stick.

SMUGGLING

William was walking quickly through Dublin airport from arrivals. He had two weighty sacks slung from his shoulders and he was in a hurry. The flight had just landed, but a luggage loading delay at Tenerife airport resulted in an extra three hours spent on the ground there. William only had bags that he stowed in the cabin lockers. He had mused, seated and waiting for the dawdlers to board, if all the passengers were as luggage conscious as him, he'd now be sitting in a bar enjoying a pint of the 'black Stuff' with his mate Tony, who was meeting him at Dublin airport and driving him home to Cork.

Customs officers astutely look for guilty-looking persons hurrying through the customs clearance zones, especially if a plane from the duty free Canary Islands has just landed. Customs searchers at Dublin airport have a great deal of success confiscating suitcases stuffed full of cigarettes, tobacco and spirits smuggled into the Republic. William, with the sacks slung over his shoulders, was a prime target for a search.

C.T. Cameras had picked out William as he headed towards the zones. He would have stuck out like a sore thumb without the sacks he carried. He was wearing his summer ware: Rangers top, baggy shorts cut from a Union Jack, a pink sombrero and sunglasses. Customs officers were primed to stop him, whichever exit he chose to use. In the 'Nothing to Declare' zone, a customs officer stepped in front of William, took him by an arm, and led him to a search table. A gaggle of custom officers lurking behind the table smirked, looked at William with interest.

'Remove the sacks from your shoulders,' demanded the customs officer preventing William's onward progress.

The customs officer loosened the binding securing the first bag. He looked inside. A look of sham amazement appeared on his face. He saw the bag was brimming with brand new mobile phones. He lifted out examples of Nokias, Samsung Galaxies and Huawei mobiles, all expensive gear, if bought in the republic. They were all in their boxes. Smiles lit up the faces of his colleagues. He said nothing and then opened the second bag. He found that one also stuffed with mobile phones. Believing beyond doubt that William was guilty of smuggling the phones, which he suspected were destined for resale in Ireland, North or South or on eBay, the custom officer asked, 'Can you explain to me why you need so many mobile phones?'

William looked the customs officer straight in the eye and told him, 'I was on holiday in Los Christianos. I got a telephone call from my mate in Cork. He said he was starting a traditional jazz band and could I please fetch him home two sacks o' phones.'

THE GREAT BRITISH TUG OF WAR BULLETIN

Past winners of this event please take note that, following on from our amazing viewer attraction "Strictly Come Wanking", we today announce the brand new 'Great British Tug of War Event'. This new and prestigious event will appear for the first time in December, on the Flip-flop Satellite channel. Viewers will judge this contest; they will be looking for innate skills.

Finalist tuggers in the spunkfest showdown will perform on New Year's Eve. Have no fears, tuggers. Flip-flop will show the event circumspectly programmed between prime shows on terrestrial channels; namely, the Hogmanay not-to-be-missed shows 'It's Only an Excuse' and 'The Bells'.

Back-to-back winners of 'Strictly' can again apply to contest the event. We'd love to see you perform. Ensure your inherent skills have not deteriorated meantime. In particular, we are sure viewers will relish the opportunity to scrutinise your dedication to elite wanking techniques and to wax ecstatic and corybantic at your phenomenal wrist skill and any new handiness you have added to your repertoire.

The very best tuggers will top of the bill. Many viewers will tune in just to witness the triple ejaculation, which many of you can achieve from the same erection. Only top tuggers bring this party piece to tugging contests.

Top Tuggers everywhere, please enter in good time.

CROSS-EYED SHEILA

I was on my first trip to sea as an engineer. As a 21 year old, I was a bit greener than most of my newfound sea mates were. With another first tripper, Ray, we were the butt of many windups. But that's how it was onboard deep-sea ships of the time, vessels leaving the UK on voyages of 4-5 months, or longer in many cases. Apart from windups, there was little entertainment onboard ships. Listening to BBC world news on crackling and whistling radios and reading books was it.

Of course, the ship did enter ports to discharge cargo and, when empty, load for the UK and sometimes the main ports in Europe, Antwerp, Rotterdam and Hamburg the busier ports of call.

That first trip our destination was Australia, through the Suez Canal and then across the Indian Ocean. Rumour had it we would remain on the Australian coast, discharge all the cargo and then load apples into the refrigerated holds for shipping for ports back home or in Europe. As a first tripper and new to anywhere outside the UK, the prospect of meeting different peoples excited me. I was particularly interested to hear that it was common practice for an officer to telephone the local hospital nurse's home in Aussie ports and invite nurses down to the ship for a drink and a dance in the officer's smoke room. I considered myself a virile young man and was sure to attract a girl that I could date during our short stay.

I introduced myself to Trudy, a nurse about the same age as I was. Ray wasn't as forward as I was, but at the end of the evening, he was dancing with

Sheila. Ray was a short arsed individual and Sheila towered over him. Other officers noticed that the more rum and cokes Sheila put away the more her eyes crossed. None of the other officers at the party tried their luck with Sheila.

At the end of the night, together with Ray, we walked Trudy and Sheila ashore. We found a taxi and took a ride with them back to the nurse's home. Ray found a doorway and propped Sheila up against the door for a snog. Trudy was up early, she said, and wanted to go indoors to bed. We kissed goodbye and promised to keep in touch.

Not to encroach on ray's activities in the doorway, because I could see and hear he was getting his end away, a noisy knee trembler. I stood fifty yards away and waited for him to finish.

The ship called back to the port to top up with apples for the homeward voyage. Cross-eyed Sheila was waiting on the quay. She was pregnant and named me as the father.

LOVER'S NUTS

Mike was suffering this painful and self-inflicted condition. He being a good friend, I mentioned to him some pathology of the plight and a specific route to a cure.

Many men know Lover's nuts as a distressing, male affliction. In acute cases, sexual frustration and thoughts causes the bollocks to rise from suspension to the horizontal plane and remain there until returning to their natural dangle. The dangling position doesn't return overnight or on administering a painkiller: it takes an insufferable time.

I must confess to not experiencing the condition since the few bouts stirring in my youthful bollocks. It is so long since I've had a prolonged erection; one lasting long enough to generate the persistent, agonising pain that accompanies this botheration.

In my book The Jock Connection, I decided Police Commander Dewsnap should experience the misery of bollocks ache. I attributed the onset to his wife leaving the marital bed and depriving him of any bollock emptying experiences. Because he was a police commander, the idea of a stress relieving masturbatory session immediately received rejection, it being inconsistent with the dignity of his rank. He suffered the torment as per my wishes.

I happily advised my friend, he not being a wanker, to take a trip to Thailand, where a person, perhaps dubious of gender, but skilled in the "Happy Ending" art, known of since pre-biblical times, could provide the cure and remove this persistent, torturous visitation.

Doctor Rob

THE BUSINESS OF SCREWING

Johnny wanted to screw Rebecca, a typist working in his office, but Rebecca belonged to someone else.

It had to happen. Johnny got so frustrated that he approached Rebecca and said, 'I'll give you £100 if you let me screw you.'

Rebecca said an emphatic, 'No.'

Johnny said, 'It will be over quickly. I'll throw the money on the floor, you bend down, and I will be finished by the time you pick it up. It's easy money and I heard that you like the back scuttle.

Rebecca thought for a moment. Could she possibly change her mind for money? She was a free spending girl and liked the feel of money in her purse. Suddenly, she found the financial side of the offer appealing; the extra cash she would spend on another nice dress. Rebecca said, 'I will have to consult my boyfriend before I could possibly agree.'

Rebecca called her boyfriend and told him the deal.

Her boyfriend thought for moment then responded: the money involved had turned his head. He needed a new snooker cue. Rebecca would buy it for him if he asked her nicely. 'Ask him for £200 and pick up the money quickly. He won't even be able to get his pants down and his cock out. You will have scooped up the £200 and be away laughing at him.'

Rebecca agreed and accepted the proposal so long as Johnny offered £200.

At lunch, when the office would be empty, was the agreed time for the fulfilment of the contract.

At his work, the boyfriend awaited Rebecca's call, to tell him of the successful outcome and the swindling of Johnny.

45 minutes pass. The boyfriend can wait no longer. He calls Rebecca and yells 'What the Hell took you so long?'

Rebecca replied, breathlessly 'That bastard Johnny threw down 5p coins.'

Management lesson: If you don't want anyone to screw you, always consider a business proposal in its entirety before agreeing to it.

MY LATEST FLAME

I heard some great news about an old girlfriend today. She's finally stopped smoking and I'm pleased for her.

Tomorrow, I pick up her ashes at the crematorium.

I picked up a new girlfriend recently. Her name is Madge, short for Margaret. Lads living in the town knew her as Madge the radge. Her sobriquet was what first attracted me to her. Explaining the nickname, Madge told me that 16 lads had once gangbanged her up a close. I asked her, 'How the fuck did that happen?'

She said, 'Oh, I was dead fucking lucky!'

What she seemed to imply was a most enjoyable fucking experience now seems improbable. She will not now contemplate having sex outdoors.

Women, they do change their minds, don't they? I love sex alfresco. Indoors only, she tells me. Nevertheless, we've come to an amicable compromise: we have sex through the front door letterbox!

It's a difficult position to be in, in more than one way, I tell you. Performing in the rain or whatever the weather, whilst I'm thrusting away against the plastic door is surreal, especially with the neighbours peeking through their curtains at the free porn show.

In the beginning, there was little comfort for me until I took the spring off the letterbox. Now it just flaps as if the postie was delivering loads of mail.

We liked to stay home most nights, watching TV and just curling up on the settee cuddling. Madge took a lot of interest in the films we watched. One taut thriller she turned to me and asked, 'Is that woman going to die?'

Studying the situation for a possible outcome I said, 'Judging by the size of the horse's cock I think she might!'

I didn't know Madge was dyslexic until I first got her into a bedroom. As we stripped off, she looked at me, pointed at my erect cock and said, 'I thought you told me you had at least a foot.'

I said, 'No, Madge, I told you I had athletes foot!' Foot problems run in the family. My father could have opened a cheese factory; such was the horrendous pong his feet gave off.

I took Madge for a dirty weekend to a Lake District honeymoon hotel. At check-in, we signed in Mr. and Mrs. I had placed one or two spots of confetti on our shoulders so we looked like genuine honeymooners.

We couldn't have looked out of place. The Receptionist asked, 'Do you want the bridal?'

Before I could reply Madge said, 'No, I'll hold him by the ears.'

We had a nice ensuite room. We weren't in many minutes when Madge said, I'll have a shower before we start playing at being a honeymooning couple.'

I was right up for that. I couldn't wait to have her slip under the duvet of the king-size bed. I thought Madge was a long time in the shower so I went to check if she was okay. I found her out of the shower, standing naked, straddling a mirror. Her gaze was downwards, towards the reflection. She was checking out her undercarriage.

I pushed Madge over and she fell into the bath.

'What the fuck did you do that for?' Madge hollered at me.

I pointed to the mirror and said, 'If you had fallen down there you'd never be seen again!'

When we got home, Madge dragged me down to the quacks. She was convinced I needed my premature ejaculations treated. She told the doctor that she'd been taking it on her chin for long enough and now it was getting on her tits.

I bought her one of those pug dogs, just to placate her. Even with the wonky eyes, the flat nose and all the slavers, the dog still loves her.

THE CASE OF THE MISSING MINCE

At 23:00 hours that Saturday, the Desk Sergeant at Easterhouses police station received the call that thieves had committed burglary at the home of Peregrine Mulgrew. The sergeant radioed beat constables Moriarty and Bond to attend at a house in Honeysuckle Drive. Their knock on arrival had the occupier answer the door.

In the living room, the constable's first impression was that there was dust visible on furniture, where someone had removed objects.

Constable Moriarty took out his pocket book and proceeded to question Mr. Mulgrew. 'I see you've one or two articles missing, Peregrine,' the constable said.

'Aye,' said Peregrine. By the way, you can call me Jock. Everyone does aroond here.'

'Okay, Jock, before I ask you what's missing, can you tell me how the perpetrators managed to gain entry?'

'They came in through the back door. An' the thieving bastards hae taken that an' the hinges an' ah. They just left me the hole but nae door. I cannae see it anywhere oot the back in the gairden.'

Moriarty prompted Constable Bond to check the back door.

'Ok, Jock, can you tell me what has been taken?' Moriarty asked.

'The bastards hae taken ma flat screen telly, ma sat box, ma I-pad, ma Timex long-service watch frae the cooncil, ma mobile phone, and ma sporran wae ma life savings o' twae poon, two-and-tuppence-happeny in it.'

Constable Moriarty wrote a list of stolen articles into his pocket book and then asked, is there anything else?'

'Aye,' said Jock, his eyes rolling upwards into his head, 'I had a big pan o' mince on the stove. The bastards hae shit in it and ah had tae through half o' it away!'

CRUISE ENRICHMENT

Husband and wife, Jake and Agnes, were transatlantic on a cruise together bound for ports in the USA. Neither had set foot on a seagoing vessel before. They had little idea that the Atlantic Ocean could erupt into a severe storm in hours. Signs onboard, spew bags placed on hand rails along all decks, and announcements made from the bridge that morning, told of a storm brewing. Nevertheless, they still took their morning circuits of the promenade deck as many of the elderly onboard were doing. By dinner, that evening, seas were higher and the ship was dipping into the waves crashing over the forecastle.

After dinner, Jake said to Agnes, 'We will go to the back end tonight for a breath of fresh air. A wave could soak us if we ventured to the pointy end.'

Standing at the starboard rail, looking at the raging surf and the dancing moon, a freak wave swept high along the ship's side. Breaking over the rail, it caught both Jake and Agnes, taking them off their feet. Jake, quite a bit heavier than Agnes, crashed sodden to the skin into the after rail. Agnes disappeared over the starboard rail.

The ship's captain took the ship in a wide circle, then came onto the reverse course to see if they could spot Agnes in the angry sea. After 12 hours of futile searching, the ship sailed on without spotting her.

The cruise company repatriated Jake. The captain told him if there was any news forthcoming on Agnes's discovery whilst the cruise was in progress, he would send him a text.

Two weeks passed. Jake received a text from the captain. It said; Coastguards found your wife's body. An oyster was found clinging to her arse. The pearl found in the oyster is valued at £50000. Please advise?

Jake texted back: send me the pearl and re-bait the trap.

THE SEAMSTRESS'S DILEMMA

Molly had sewn pieces of clothing together for years. Repairing family clothing and in her job in the sweatshop, she had become accomplished with needle and thread. She was a dab hand with needles of any size and could produce some fine, artistic work crocheting and embroidering.

Sitting in the good morning light of the conservatory, Molly suddenly realised she was out of cotton. The task in hand she had to finish before nightfall. Molly gripped the needle she was using between her lips and placed the work in progress on a stool. Rising from her chair, she went indoors looking for her sewing box that she had left in the kitchen.

On entering the kitchen, Molly could smell pepper in the air. It indicated to her that her husband had sprinkled the spice liberally on his breakfast eggs. Quickly, a titanic sneezing fit overwhelmed her. She could not control the seizure. Her head rocked back so violently that the needle shot from her lips and disappeared over her throat.

The thought of the sharp-pointed needle puncturing her intestines worried Molly. She realised that the Accident and Emergency department of the local hospital would have the perfect answer to this type of problem. How surgeons removed needles from intestines was beyond her knowledge.

At the A&E, Molly saw a mature looking doctor. He listened intently to what she had to say about the occurrence.

The doctor looked at Molly intently, then smiled and said, 'Molly, there's nothing to worry you. The needle will pass in a natural bodily function.'

Molly enquired, 'What if my husband and I are having sexual intercourse when the needle is passing?'

'Get him to wear a thimble,' the doctor advised.

THE STRETCH EXPLAINED

Vanessa had retired from 'the game'. She no longer wanted or needed to earn a living as a brass, to prostitute her body for the pleasure of men. A normal life was what she wanted for the remainder of her life. Although she was still attractive facially, after many years working at her tiring profession, she doubted that she would meet a man who would provide her with the happiness she so desired.

Darby had a posh name. He always seemed to be sitting next to her in the quiet snug bar where she ritually went to imbibe an afternoon gin and tonic before dinner. Darby had often offered to take her out to a posh restaurant for dinner, but she had refused the offers.

Vanessa thought Darby was younger than she was. From their conversations, she had learned that he retired early, at the age of 45, as Met Police inspector, had never married, had a good pension and lived in Wanstead.

Vanessa had to make a choice: was it to be Darby with whom she threw in her lot.

Vanessa came to a quick decision. She finally accepted Darby's offer of dinner. Within weeks, the besotted Darby proposed marriage. Vanessa accepted; however, acceptance worried her. Her vagina was to some extent oversized following 25 years in her previous occupation. Not to jeopardise the chance of happiness, she decided that she would broach the subject after the marriage ceremony.

On honeymoon, Vanessa explained that, as a child raised in the country, she had accidently caught her fanny on a barbed wire fence when she had tried to clamber over it, which was why her fanny was as big as it was.

Undismayed, Darby put all his energy into wild lovemaking sessions, taking Vanessa in various positions throughout the night.

In the morning as they lay together, Darby said, 'I can understand your fanny being somewhat stretched by snagging up on barbed wire, but tell me, dear heart, just how far across the field were you before you noticed!

LOTTERY OF LIFE

The last words Dermot said to his wife Coleen that Saturday afternoon, before he left the house to start the late turn 4 o'clock to midnight shift at the nearby hotel bar, 'Don't forget to enter my line in tonight's lottery.'

Coleen, replied, 'You know me Dermot. I'm out shopping to the supermarket. I'll do that then.'

Every Saturday, the bar was busy, especially in the evening when the City's piss artists and revellers with their girlfriends in tow descended on the bar in great numbers. Dermot had told colleen never to phone him on a Saturday. He'd be run off his feet was the reason he gave her.

At 10 o'clock, hotel reception put a call from Coleen through to the bar for Dermot. The bar manager picked up the phone when it started ringing. He signalled Dermot that the call was for him, and said as he passed, 'It's from your wife,' whilst conveying by his facial grimacing that he was displeased with the disruption. Dermot answering the call would mean one less hand serving at the busy bar.

Dermot spoke into the phone mouthpiece, 'I thought I told you never to ring me at work.'

Coleen replied, sounding flustered, 'It's about the six lottery numbers you asked me to put on this afternoon. It's bad news, worse news, but at the end of the day, it's not bad news at all, at all.'

'Go on; tell me the bad news, 'Dermot said, wondering what the hell the woman was talking about.

'I forgot to put your six numbers on!' Coleen said, hesitatingly.

'Bejasus,' Dermot erupted, 'what's the worse fucking news,' guessing what Coleen would tell him next.

'Your 6 numbers were drawn tonight,' Coleen told him quickly.

Dermot had guessed correctly, then, in an agitated state asked, 'How the fuck can there be any good news after hearing what you've just told me?'

Coleen replied, 'There was nothing to worry about. Tonight, there were no winners!'

A TOWN WITHOUT

The time is nigh. I must decide which tavern bar sees my coin slide over its slopping top. The watering hole must suit my pocket. My pennies must cover my choice of warming nectar without an embarrassing 'sling your hook' retort. I do not care to cram the purse of them who offer pricey drink.

The tavern of my choice must also provide for my discernment young, desirable, serving wenches. They must be buxom with titties that don't droop like wax sagging down the length of a prayer candle. They must also boast bottoms firm, rounded, muscular and strong, not broad like the stern of a canal barge, evidence of many births. They must flaunt their cuddlesome, huggable derrières so haunting in dreams; ensuring nocturnal ejaculation comes easy and often, with pleasure. Many mornings I have awakened stuck to stiff sheets, on arising hearing cussing from the lips of the serving wenches of the lodgings I use.

The wenches must also be honest and deliver my correct change in small and delicate hands. Hands in which I can picture my cock laid, looking large and proud, grasped eagerly by tender fingers. Their nails, manicured neatly, no raggedness inflicted dragging brimming pisspots along rough flooring from beneath sagging beds, to leave on my cock telltale scrapes or ulcerating scars.

My mind races over the choices of tavern available in this disreputable town. Is there a hostelry to suit my desires? Sadly, none comes to mind quickly. I must wander on down that road, seeking that illusive, happy place.

Fellow wayfarers I meet tramping on my eternal perambulation I will ask, in which town did hostelries receive them well. Can they recommend a tavern where the taking of their pittance was not the sole object of the greedy taverner? Did serving wenches fuck them better? Were they clean? Were they pleasing in their sexual knowledge? Did they pass on any incurable pox? After the fucking, were they guilt-free in their minds? Perhaps, I will never find this special place. I will never meet you there: not in this town.

BEGGING

Barak was poor even by beggar standards. He did not possess a stitch of clothing. What he had once possessed, other beggars had stripped from his body, whilst he was recovering from binging on neat Ouzo, sleeping it off by the side of a rock. When he awoke from his alcoholic slumbers, he found his body naked and regretted purloining Ouzo by theft from a wayside grog shop?

The beggars had moved on. Barak had no hope of finding the perpetrators and even if he did, how could he identify his rags. He was now condemned to begging in towns and villages naked. He felt like an idiot, but he had to move on, preferably clothed, to cover the twelve inches of his penis, but he needed Drachma to replace the basic rags he had lost. He cried out as he walked 'Bring out your paper and rags,' his words ignored, deaf ears everywhere.

Trudging through his tenth village of the morning, imploring the village folk to bring out their unwanted paper and rags, Barak halted in his tracks on hearing the dulcet voice of a woman shouting from high up, 'My man.'

Barak looked around then up towards a nearby balcony. There he saw a plain looking woman standing, a feather duster in her hand. Seeing she had attracted Barak's attention, the woman said, 'Come up the stairs and see me.'

Barak found the door to the apartment, knocked and entered. The woman had undressed and was lying on a straw filled mattress, legs wide. 'Take me, my man, with your massive cock,' she begged him.

In the early evening, feeling weary after his day with the woman, Barak was still naked and back on the road through the village, with nowhere to put the few coins she had given him. His imploring had changed by a word: paper, rags, fucking, paper, rags, fucking.

THE SEIKO WATCH

Roddy and Tommy met in the play park. Both were addicted to swings, often egging each other on to greater heights, trying to impress the gaggle of young lassies they knew from school. On a passing, a sleeve of Tommy's jacket rode up, revealing a Seiko watch on his left arm.

Roddy's feet hit the ground. He scuffed his shoes along until the swing stopped. 'When did you get that new watch,' he asked Tommy, 'it's a beauty.'

Tommy put his feet down and stopped his swing. 'Saturday morning,' he said excitedly, 'my dad was off work and as I crept past my parent's bedroom door I could hear the grunting and groaning of them having sex. I opened the bedroom door and just stood there. Dad must have heard me because he turned his head and roared at me "Get out and you can have anything you want." I want a Seiko watch,' I told him. That's how I got it. Dad keeps looking at me funny now.'

Roddy replied, 'I'd love a watch like that. Next time my dad's off on a Saturday; I'm going to hang about my parent's bedroom door in the morning to see if I can hear them at it.'

The first Saturday his dad was off work, Roddy was up early to hang about outside his parent's bedroom door, hoping to hear them at it and to secure a watch. Sure enough, beyond the door the bedsprings started creaking slowly, then faster. He thought he could hear his mother speaking in a strange language, something akin to Swahili. Roddy opened the door and walked to the foot of the bed. His dad was on top of his mother, both beneath the duvet. His dad turned his head and shouted, 'What the fuck do you want?'

Roddy stammered, 'I wanna watch.'

His dad shouted back, 'Sit on that stool in the corner and keep quiet!'

WITNESS TO MURDER

Norman woke up, the bedroom dark, the fluorescent face of the clock on the bedside table said 03:19. He had drunk quite a few pints with his pals down the pub the previous evening. Now his bladder felt pressed up. He would need to get out of the warm bed and grope his way around the bedroom to the toilet. He didn't want to put on a light, disturb his wife, and hear her moans that he had awakened her. He'd heard enough grief from her before he went to bed about his drunken state on returning from the pub.

Passing the bedroom window looking out over the garden, Norman thought he heard a shed door close. He pulled the curtain to one side and looked out. Street lighting illuminated his next-door neighbour, in pyjamas, crouched behind his garden shed. He held a shovel, the bladed end high in his hands. Norman presumed the neighbour was ready to strike someone or something lurking in the shed.

The shed door opened and a burglar emerged, pushing the neighbour's moped. Norman recognised him. He disliked him intensely. The burglar was the thief who had broken into his shed and had stolen his bicycle. He had seen him riding it in the street. He hadn't reported it to police as he was going to dish out his own brand of retribution when an opportunity occurred.

The neighbour leapt out from his hiding place and launched the metal end at the burglar's head. Norman gasped as he saw the burglar's head leave his body, somersault a couple of times, then fall to the ground.

The neighbour then began to dig a hole in his vegetable patch. When he returned from the toilet, Norman peeked through the curtains. He saw the neighbour pulling the burglar by the legs towards the hole.

Norman's gasp woke his wife. 'Get back into bed you drunken bugger,' she admonished him.

'You will never believe what I've just seen, Norman said. 'That tosser next door still has the shovel loaned him.'

THE WEDDING RECEPTION RIOT EXPLAINED

Judge Tavish McTavish had never heard such rowdiness in his court. He thumped his gavel onto the reinforced portion of his bench and called out, 'Order in court, order in court.' No one in the public gallery took any notice of his order. The noise of arguments continued. It was clear to Tavish that the two families involved in the disturbance in his court were the same families that were the subjects of the police charges. Charges of serious assaults that followed a serious outbreak of violence at a wedding reception held in the town.

Tavish was unsure that proceedings could get underway until he cleared the court. If he didn't, he might have to suspend them to a future date, hoping there would be a settlement of differences between the protagonist families. Then he saw a man walk towards the bench and whispered to the court clerk. The clerk rose and bent over the bench and spoke to Tavish.

'Silence in court. Would Dempsey Flanagan please take the stand,' Tavish said loudly. He hoped what Dempsey had to say would resolve the situation that hadn't quietened.

Dempsey took the stand and said to the court, 'I was best man to the groom. He and I have known each other since our schooldays. I believe I can clear up for you exactly why the uproar at the wedding reception occurred.

'Carry on,' said Tavish, pleased that at last the proceedings were getting somewhere.

115

Dempsey began his story: 'It is traditional at most wedding receptions that the best man has the first dance with the bride. It certainly was in our town. I approached the bride as the band struck up for that first dance and asked for her hand in the waltz. Smiling, the bride agreed, as I expected her to do, and we took to the floor. Both families cheered. We finished the waltz and the band quickly struck up again, this time with a slow foxtrot. The bride was smiling generously. I could tell she was enjoying dancing with me. That dance finished and the band quickly struck up with a quickstep. We continued to dance. After the eighth dance, I reckoned we'd been dancing together for half an hour. Then judge, the cause of the disturbance happened. The groom leapt from the top table, raced onto the dance floor, and kicked his bride in the fanny.

'Wow,' Tavish said, wiping his forehead with a towel, 'that must have been painful.

'It bloody well was,' Dempsey said, 'he broke three of my fingers!'

SUPERMARKET SWEAT

Roger was on shared maternity leave. His wife Ruby was heavily pregnant with their second child. That was why he had chosen to go shopping on his own to the supermarket that Saturday morning: he intended to use his free time usefully and didn't want anyone bumping into Ruby's bump, whilst she pushed a trolley along the isles.

He had a long shopping list that included requirements for the expected baby. Nappies, bottom lotion, gripe water and feed bottles were top of the list and he had scoured the isles to find them. Shopping as per the list had taken some time.

Approaching the checkout, Roger saw an attractive woman trying to attract his attention. She was about the same age as he was, but he could not figure out if he had met her before, perhaps Ruby was a friend. Nevertheless, he pushed the trolley towards her and took hold of the hand she outstretched and gave it a quick shake. 'Do you know me?' Roger asked.

The woman replied, 'You're the father of one of my kids.'

In shock, Roger's mind raced back to the only time he has ever been unfaithful to Ruby. It had happened when she was his fiancée. He asked the woman, 'Are you the stripper from my bachelor party that I had sex with on the pub pool table, with all my mates watching and egging me on, while your partner raised weals and blisters on my arse when she whipped me?'

The woman said, looking deeply upset, 'No, I'm your son's schoolteacher!'

117

THAT BLOODY CAT'S BACK

True, it was a shock when the mother-in-law's toes suddenly curled, connecting big time with the pail. It was a further shock when my missis, Sadie, and I realised she was uninsured and we had to fork out for the funeral. Cremation was the cheapest option so we took the old girl one last journey down that route. Her final journey was back to our mantelpiece in a cardboard urn.

Sadie's mum had lived in a council house for years. Her furniture was tat, old; nobody wanted any of it so we paid a white-van man to cart it to the rubbish tip. I wasn't too pleased coughing up for that outcome, either.

The only heirloom bequeathed to us was her manky, straggly-haired ginger cat. I was sure she had a touch of lion in her makeup, but she boasted the most popular name in moggiedom: Kitty.

Of course, Kitty took to Sadie; seemed to hate me. Whenever I wanted to sit next to Sadie, on the settee, to snuggle close, share a bottle of wine or watch TV, Bloody Kitty leapt between us and wouldn't budge her feline backside. Kitty was asking for trouble!

When she brought her noxious anal gland with its oily, stinking chemical warfare onto the battlefield to attack me, move me from my rightful place next to my missis, it was the final straw.

The first opportunity to get rid of the beast, I promised myself I'd take.

That occasion arose one Friday night. It was usual that Sadie ironed shirts and stuff so that I had something to look smart wearing down the pub of a weekend night. A couple of pints with my mates were my only relaxation outside the home of any week; small reward for my job heaving wheelie bins onto the hoist at the back of the garbage truck.

Kitty was lying happily asleep, purring gently on my settee spot. She could have been dreaming of sexual molestation by one of the marauding Tomcats stalking the alleyways near our house after dark. An abdominal scar showed she had had been spayed, but I didn't know if she got laid regular, when she left the house late at night. Perhaps she just went to perform her ablutions or mouse. More likely, she was planning her next attack on me, armed with something akin to Agent Orange, phosgene or mustard gas.

I snatched up an Aldi bag from the kitchen, crept close to Kitty, picked her up by her neck scruff and rammed her into the bag, before she realised what was happening.

Out the back door I flew, tying a knot in the bag as I went, sealing Kitty inside. My car was a Volkswagen Beetle, the one with the boot up front. I unlatched the boot lid and tossed in the bag, making sure it bounced a couple of times before it hit the back. I heard a loud, painful squeal. It pleased me.

There were big acreage fields not five minutes from our house. I considered one of them *the* ideal place to dump this germ-warfare exponent. In the potato field, the shaws were high, but the drills I could walk easily along until I quickly reached the field middle.

I dumped the bag there, unopened, leaving the beast to perish. Perhaps a fox or dog would rip the bag open and tear Kitty to pieces, slowly. I wished I'd taken a spade with me. A small burial would have gone unnoticed.

Back home ten minutes later, I pushed open the living room door to find Sadie sitting on the settee with Kitty, looking not the least discontented, laid across her lap.

How she had escaped and returned home safely as quickly I couldn't work out. I was stunned.

Other opportunities would arise, I was sure; next time I'd use a stronger bag, secure it better and the dumping site would be at least ten miles from our house.

When Sadie took a bath, she usually languished in it, reading a book for at least an hour, topping up with hot water to keep warm. Early Sunday evening was her usual time and I prepared for a Sabbath moggienapping.

The bags the council sell for 50p a go for householders in which to collect additional rubbish are extra strong. If I doubled the bags up, tied the beast's legs up with Gaffa tape, surely there would be no escape from my next attempt.

Early evening, Kitty had drifted off, her light snores catching my hearing. A simple snatch and a quick flick around the front paws with a length of the tape trapped her. I even wrapped some tape around her jaws for good measure, ensuring she couldn't bite her way out, as it seems she must have done that the last time.

In the bag, she did a bit of birling, but no claws broke through. On hitting the rear of the boot with a resounding thump, I imagined, but for the tape clamping her meowing jaws together, she screamed in pain, such was the strength in my throw as I hurled her onto the hard metal surface.

I drove like crazy, swinging the car around bends, giving Kitty the last 'ride of her life', rattling her from side to side off the metalwork. A wood, some 10 miles distance, was my destination.

I had the Gaffa tape with me. I scrambled through the twilight of the wood. Near its centre, I found a tree with a branch just above head height. I lashed the bag to it; there was no movement inside. Kitty might be dead already. I wished. Then I safely made my way out, without breaking my neck tripping over twisted and raised root formations.

As I parked up outside our house, the bathroom light was out, the bedroom light on. Sadie would dry herself off there, dress in a nightgown and lash on some 'I'll make you want me' perfume, before joining me on the settee. Sunday used to be our lovemaking night. We had always looked forward to these sessions. Then Kitty arrived. Her foul-smelling squirting, every time I'd tried to get close to Sadie, would put a skunk off any form of sexual activity.

Now I had accomplished mission impossible. I'd rid the house of Kitty. Tonight could be a night to remember.

As I entered the hallway, Sadie was halfway down the stairs, Kitty in her arms, some whiskers missing where she had torn the tape off her face.

The sight dropped my jaw. I was flabbergasted.

I was more determined than ever that Kitty had to go. The cat was making an absolute fool out of me. However, only I knew that, and I wasn't about to share the information with anyone.

Each Wednesday, evening session, Sadie went to the bingo with pals. An afternoon telephone call for Sadie confirmed the venue for that night. I considered her lengthy absence would give me the opportunity to drive far from the beaten track.

I marshalled my thoughts: somewhere up a fell, in the Lake District, 60 miles from Annan, at least, would be an appropriate, out-of-the-way location, dumping site, from where an unwanted moggie couldn't possibly find its way home.

The second hand shop had a strong and secure cat-proof-looking holdall. I bought it cheaply, secreting it in the car boot. The small lock I kept in a pocket. There'd be no escape next time.

Wednesday evening at 6p.m., Sadie's lift arrived. I'd have at least 4 hours to get to my destination and be home before her. I was in trapping mode by 6.05 p.m.

Kitty was sitting contentedly on the settee as I approached her. She stood up, arched her back, raised her hackles and bared her teeth as she viewed my intent. I held the holdall open-side down and leapt towards her, pushing it down over her, securing her within. The zip closed easily and the lock clicked into place sharply: job done.

Further map reading had pointed me in the direction of the River Derwent as an ideal dumping site. The river flowed towards the Irish Sea, rising from the small Styhead tarn, high in the Lake District. I memorised the route to get to the tarn from an old map. I would take the M6 as far as Penrith, then turn west along the A66 towards the Lakes, then the B5289 into the hills.

The Derwent tumbled through Borrowdale Valley, before entering Derwentwater, continued westwards, through Lake Bassenthwaite and out into the Isel Valley. The Derwent flowed from the Lake

District to Cockermouth, the River Cocker joining there, adding to the already significant stream. I considered a voyage of this magnitude was enough to confuse any cat with senses limited so entombed, if it had not already drowned in a waterlogged holdall, before swirling out into the Irish Sea at Workington.

This was the ultimate one-way ticket for any unwanted moggie, of that I was sure!

By 8 p.m., I was high in the Lakeland fells, on the track to the tarn. Swinging round a bend, I saw the small stretch of water ahead. I travelled along its edge until I saw a bridge. Beneath the bridge, tarn water left in a strong cascade, splashing over glistening rocks. It was not quite in an impressive waterfall yet, but crashing noises coming from around the bend, up ahead, hinted of a stronger flow there, possibly over a high escarpment.

I swung the holdall around my head 50 times, enough to stun any moggie head blessed with innate, home-finding abilities, then dropped it into the gurgling water to watch it plummet away and disappear beneath a covering of foam.

It got dark quickly and I still cannot remember where I took the wrong turning. At 10 p.m., I was in a cul-de-sac: an old slate quarry at the end of some godforsaken trail, Herdwick sheep all around, watching me, bemusedly.

'I panicked, that's for sure. I checked my mobile to see if it had a signal. It was weak, but it was there. I rang home. Sadie answered. 'Is Kitty there,' I asked.

'Yes, she's here. However, I think she has been out fighting with the Toms. All her claws are missing and her paws are raw. She has no whiskers. Some teeth are missing, as is one ear. She looks a bit wet, confused and angry to me.'

'Can you put her on the phone for me?' I asked, 'I'm lost!'

Indian Street Practitioners

A Personal View

I have personally witnessed scores of Indian ear cleaning practitioners working at their profession, as the year nears its end. During the December festival of the Lughole Cleaning, the hearing-impaired-by-dust-and-wax patients form queues along the pavements of cities, towns and villages, to have local exponents perform this necessary, annual task.

Quite obviously, India being a dustbowl and the Asian Indian the best producers of earwax on that continent, there's lumps of work on the pavements of Mumbai, where the photographer took this picture.

However, as I watched it became apparent that these executors of the lughole cleanout had a secret: they could clean out both ears from one side of the head. Unbelievable, I know, but it seems ancient lughole cleansing gurus taught their protégée artisans the location of the secret tunnel running between the ear canals of each lughole. Now that's productivity in my book and why industry on the Indian continent is leaving us behind in so many ways.

Another little-known Indian-street consultant is the 'Boil Sucker'. This is a more ancient and needful art, performed only by men. The boil can be a painful plague to the skins of us all, but the Asian Indian suffers most. I have also seen boil suckers in action; indeed, it's a gut-wrenching sight to behold.

Typically, the boil sucker uses a hollowed out length of bamboo to perform the operation. The boil sucker requests the patient to reveal the location of the boil, sensitive areas included. To jog your memory to a boil's appearance: it has a red and bluish base, very painful looking and intensely so to the touch, with a crimson, volcanic stack, upon which rests the yellow, Korma-coloured, suppurating tip not quite ready to erupt.

The boil located and sized, the boil sucker selects a bamboo pipe with a suitable inner diameter from an array of such instruments suitable for treating anything from a zit to the dreaded, double-headed carbuncle.

At this point, the boils sucker offers the boil bearer the opportunity to take, for a few extra Rupees, a piece of seasoned teak to grip between teeth whilst the procedure takes place. Few sufferers refuse this offer.

The teak placed and gripped solidly between teeth is the cue for the process to begin. The boil sucker places the bamboo tube over the boil, then presses it downwards to ensure a good seal. The patient screams, slavers fly from his lips. Teeth crunch onto the teak. Sweat flows from the brows of both the boil sucker and the patient.

The boils sucker places the other end of the bamboo tube into his mouth. His lips close about the tube, much in the manner a Venus flytrap plant as it traps a victim. He breathes several times through his nostrils. He evacuates his lungs. His ribcage shrinks to half its original size.

His cheeks sink inwards as the evacuation of the boil commences. The opposite inner linings of his mouth touch. The bamboo tube begins to creak as the vacuum increases. Teeth crumble in the boil-bearer's head as both gums attempt to meet at teak centre.

One minute into the procedure and the boil sucker's eyes have enlarged, are forcing out of their sockets. The boil-bearer has become unconscious, his teeth littering the pavement like a scattering of shattered, curry-stained pearls. The boil is now two-thirds of the way up the bamboo tube, inexorably on its way out the top.

Then there is a sound, much like that of an elephant removing a foot from quicksand and the boil sucker's head rocks backwards, the bamboo pipe, released from its suction, leaps from the operation site.

As the boil sucker turns his head looking for his next patient, he spits the contents of the boil into the gutter, where hungry vermin and vultures fight over it. Stretcher-bearers, always on standby, cart the patient away to the recovery suite, a swept clean pavement around the corner.

I saw it, I swear.

SHITEHAWK LIMIES BAND

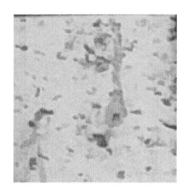

Knowledge of the Liverpool blues-rock recording band Shitehawk Limies' early years, when known simply as Hawk, and yet to perform at the world-renowned Liverpool venue The Cavern, has remained hidden from the world until now. Recently published annals reveal that the earliest musical inspirations and their later name choice occurred to band members on a visit to Lime Street Station.

For decades, rumours circulating Liverpool's musician groups suggested that a strong hum emanated from the Lime Street Station Gents. Keen to pursue a new musical direction, the easily influenced Shitehawk Limies quintet of Weasel, Stoat, Rat, Skunk and Dingo, they were a bunch of fucking animals, really, sniffed around the popular bog on many a Sunday afternoon. The quintet of average musicians absorbed the musical nuances circulating in that foul atmosphere. It would make their band famous in Iraq.

Their unique style of music turned the band into the greatest band sound ever to send Baghdadian youth crazy for blues and rock music. Baghdadis shed their kaftans and hijabs, donned jeans and Shitehawk Limies' T-shirts, lifted a sandy flip-flop and jived to the new, incredible, throbbing, heavy-bass line, blues-rock beat.

It was during Sabbath excursions to this famous temple that Lime Street has become, that ideas materialised for numbers to include in Shitehawk Limies seminal album; namely, Windy on the roof and Vanguff's Picturesque Droppings.

High in the station roof, a glass panel revealed seagulls doing something the species did with regularity: shit in spectacular fashion. Band members named a pair of frequently alighting seagulls. Windy spread her droppings on the glass in an interesting, but unfathomable assortment. Vanguff was more sophisticated in his execution; he bombed deposits in many-pronged attacks of sheer class onto the glass. On closer inspection, Vanguff is responsible for building onto the glass the outlines of an earless face. Art critics acknowledge Vanguff's work as one of the finest example of avian art.

I'm sure, in droppings encrusted indelibly onto the glass roofs of other great temples, and the hum emanating from many of their bogs, art historians will perceive examples of inspirations yet undiscovered.

NO DAY TRIP

In the days before steam, Horatio yearned for a life on the ocean wave, dreamed of sailing to all of those faraway places with strange sounding names. When he was 16 years-old, he left home with his parent's blessing and headed for Bristol, the nearest port as the crow flies. The captain of tea clipper loading general cargo for the Indian Subcontinent liked the cut of Horatio's jib and signed him on for the long voyage around the Cape of Good Hope.

Horatio learned quickly that the clipper would only stop at ports in-between Bristol and Calcutta, to take aboard fresh water and stores. He wondered, the cutter being so long at sea, how the crew relieved themselves sexually, there being no shore leave to meet dusky maidens and release a build up of bodily juices.

The captain was walking on deck, the first day at sea. Horatio approached him and asked, 'Captain, there are no women onboard, no shore leave in port, so how do crew relieve themselves on such a long voyage.

The captain was a genial soul from Devon. With a twinkle in his eye, he said to Horatio, 'See yonder door in the mast-house under the forward mast. Well here's the key. Go ahead and open the door. Make sure you close it behind you. In the mast-house, you will find a barrel. The barrel has a hole in it. Take the bung from the hole and stick in your cock. I guarantee you will have a lovely, satisfying time. I'm sure you will find this arrangement satisfactory for your needs.

Horatio took the key, opened the door beneath the mast and entered. He closed the door behind him. It was dark but he found the barrel, spotted the bung, which he removed. He had no need to wait for an erection to develop: he had been nursing one since coming onboard. He stuck his cock into the hole. It was wonderful and warm in there. With the impetuosity of his youth, Horatio had three thrusts against the barrel and he had spilled his lot in record time.

Horatio asked the captain for the mast house key 6 nights in a row. On the 7th night, the captain refused to hand over the key. 'Why is that?' Horatio asked, sounding upset.

The captain said, with a gleam in his eyes, 'Laddie, tonight it is your turn in the barrel!'

ALL IN A VET'S DAY

Richard Dickson was a veterinarian surgeon. A major responsibility of his was treating the ills cattle and other beasts suffered on the farms of the Cumbrian hills. He had just experienced a hell of a day out on the fells, a blistering wind blowing. Two miles from a main road, a sizeable Charolais bull had entangled itself in a barbed wire fence. The bull was running amok, crazed, dragging a good portion of the fence behind it.

Richie, as the farming fraternity knew him, rode to the hillside field on a Gator Utility Vehicle alongside the farmer. He had to shoot a dart of sedatives into the bull to sedate the angered beast on arrival. Then he had to wrestle it free of the barbed wire, without enmeshing himself in the barbs. The bull had several wounds that he later had to dress.

Richie had telephoned home before he left the site. He spoke to his wife Dolly and told her that he would be arriving home late. He also described briefly, what had kept him on the fells.

When he arrived home, it was past 9pm. Dolly was there waiting with a cool bottle of Theakston's Old Peculiar already poured into a goblet. He took a sip of the dark beer and then hurried into the shower room to remove the animal stench sticking to him.

On an earlier foray that week into the Cumbrian hills, a farmer had presented him with a leg of Hardwick lamb. He could smell the aroma of the roast as Dolly removed it from the oven. With a glass of Bordeaux red, he knew he had a meal to enjoy waiting.

Imbibing the Old Peculiar and most of the bottle of Bordeaux over dinner had made Richie yawn. At 11pm, he took to the stairs to bed, leaving Dolly to clear up the dinner plates. He was well asleep when Dolly slipped beneath the duvet. He didn't notice her arrival.

About 2pm, Richie turned in bed and felt Dolly's warm body next to him. He snuggled up close to her, lifted her nightie, revealed her ample bare buttocks, then moved closer. Dolly felt Richie's presence and his erection behind her. She woke up immediately and let out a moan of pleasure. Richie new she was receptive to a spot of lovemaking. He was pleased he had awakened when he did.

At the most pleasurable moment of lovemaking, the bedside telephone began to ring. Dolly picked up the handset and held the earpiece to her head for a moment. The voice of an elderly woman kept repeating, 'Is this the vets?'

Dolly passed the handset behind her to Richie. 'It's for you,' she said.

'This is the vet,' Richie said into the mouthpiece. 'Is this an emergency?' he asked in his most demanding voice.

'Well, sort of,' the woman said, 'there's a whole bunch of cats on the roof outside my bedroom window, making a terrible noise. It's a mating frenzy, and I can't get to sleep. What can I do about it?'

Richie took a sharp intake of breath. Then he patiently said. 'Open the window and tell them they're wanted on the phone.'

'Really, the woman said, 'Will that that stop them?'

'It should do, Richie said, 'It sure stopped me.'

Eye, Eye

The public bar of the General Havelock pub was quiet that morning. Donald was sitting at one end of the bar supping away at a pint of Guinness when a well-dressed woman wearing a beret entered the pub and sat at the opposite end of the bar. He heard the woman ask the barman for a gin and tonic with ice and slice. She pulled a wallet from her handbag, chose a card from it and placed it on the bar.

Donald had sat for a good twenty minutes since the woman entered. She had not once peered in his direction.

He rattled the bar with a coin to attract the barman's attention. The barman had stood for a while polishing the same glass whilst engaging the woman in conversation. Donald's coin rattle worked. The barman picked up a clean pint pot, walked towards him and nodded towards the Guinness font. Donald noticed the woman turn her head to look down the bar top in his direction. She was popping crisps into her mouth at the same time. She probably wanted a better look at him, he thought.

Suddenly, the woman threw her had back and let rip an enormous sternutation, a succession of sneezes of colossal proportions. Another rattle on the bar top attracted Donald's attention. A glass eye was bouncing its way along the bar towards him. He stretched out a hand when the eye was close enough and caught it before it shot over the bar-top edge onto the floor. He looked at the woman. When she stopped sneezing, he could tell that she had a vacant eye socket.

Donald rose from his stool and walked quickly towards the woman, careful not to trip on the rough floor Linoleum. Within reach of her, he stretched out an arm to display the eye sitting safely in his hand. With a hand over her vacant socket, she dismounted from the stool, peered closely at his hand and delicately picked up the eye. She had a glass-eye washing kit in her handbag, which she took out, opened, sprayed the eye from an aerosol and wiped it dry as he stood there. Then she slipped the eye back into the socket in a well-practiced manoeuvre.

Seated and settled, the woman said, to Donald, 'What a gentleman, I must buy you a drink. What will be your pleasure, a gin and tonic or a nice malt whisky?

'Nothing for me. I just happened to be sitting where the eye rolled.

'Nonsense. Have a drink with me. I'm Doris. Fetch your stool along and join me.'

Time seemed to fly by. Drink flowed. Doris would not allow Donald to buy a drink, although he tried hard to coax her. At 2 pm Doris said to Donald, 'I'm heading home now. I just live around the corner in the Spectrum Tower Block. I would like you to see me home, make sure I get there. Will you?'

'If you insist,' Donald said. 'I'm not going too far this afternoon.'

Doris opened the door of her apartment and pulled Donald inside. She walked him directly into the bedroom and began to strip off. Donald stood watching Doris, gawping.

'Don't be shy, I'm not,' Doris said, 'we can have a lovely afternoon beneath my duvet. What are you waiting for?'

Donald shrugged his jacket off, tossed it onto a bedside chair, sat down on the bed and untied his shoelaces. Doris crawled over the bed to him and helped him remove his shirt and tie, slipped his braces off his shoulders, pulled him back, caught hold of his trouser legs and yanked the trousers off. The afternoon of lovemaking was ace.

Donald said to Doris, 'I'm an ugly little runt really. So why did you fancy me?'

Doris said, 'You just caught my eye!'

FINISHING SCHOOL

Raymond Tripper farmed a thousand acres of prime land in County Antrim. His farm equipment and his steading were modern and his farmhouse outstanding; the envy of his neighbours, top quality, and the best money could buy. Many of his neighbouring contemporaries thought him a millionaire, but he was too modest ever to brag that they had guessed correctly.

His only child, his daughter Magdalene, was sixteen. She was bright and beautiful, dressed sensibly, turned many a head at the Young Farmer Club barn dances held in the county.

Raymond had to make a decision on his daughter's future. Could it be a degree course at Belfast's reputable Queens University? Could he find for her an institution that would train her for a mannerly life, give her the social courtesy she would not find in her present locality?

Switzerland had the reputation of finishing the education of royal children. At a prestigious school there, she would meet other young women of breeding. Though he had done well, built up his farm to the envy of other farmers in the county, he could not countenance his daughter taking up a farmer's hard life.

Switzerland was his choice. Scouring the internet, he found the ideal school in Lausanne. It had the curriculum and a client list that brought joy to his heart. Magdalene would return home after two years there a perfect lady.

Magdalene was a bit anxious that her father had chosen her future unwisely, but she succumbed to his whim and flew quite happily out of Belfast airport to begin the next two years of her life.

Magdalene wrote home every week, updating her parents on her progress and mentioning the names of some of her new friends. In her first letter home, she pointed out to her parents that they had misspelled her first name and that tutors had taught her that Magdalene was the correct spelling.

The first year passed quickly. Magdalene was due home. Then her letter arrived that shook Raymond to the core. Magdalene had met a French Count and was going to marry him and bring him home to meet her parents.

In a rage, Raymond wrote back. Come home alone immediately. I'm not wasting any more of my hard-earned money if the school cannot teach you to spell correctly.

RIDING A BIKE WITHOUT LIGHTS
HAS ITS DANGERS

Because of overcrowding, within Cape Town's Pollsmoor prison, the system incarcerated Afrikaners Jacobus and Janco with Bandile, a Bantu tribesman. They had never met before, in or out of prison. Their conversations ranged from home life to the crimes they had committed.

Jacobus relating the significant aspects of his crime said, 'Man, I got 5 years for a minor assault. The judge said I was lucky to get away with the minor charge, as this prison is a mess, overcrowding the problem. Had the police alleged ABH, he'd put me away for 10.'

Janco had a similar story to tell. 'I'd had a few drinks and was driving home to Walmer Estate when a black guy, crazy on the weed, lurched off the sidewalk and landed underneath the wheels of my car. Both front and back went over him. I made a good job of it. Because I'd been drinking the judge gave me 15 years. He said if I'd killed a white man, he'd have given me 25.'

Bandile had a very different account of his incarceration, 'I was riding my bike to work down the Mojo market at Sea Point. I sweep up the litter there. The cops stopped me for riding the bike without lights. I can count myself lucky that the judge only gave me 55 years.'

Both Jacobus and Janco erupted together, 'How the fuck was that lucky?'

Bandile replied, 'The judge said if I'd been riding the bike during the hours of darkness he would have hung me!'

SAVED FROM THE BARREL

Raleigh thought the Christian name his parents had baptised him with was reason enough for him to consider a seagoing career. At 18 years of age, he was a strapping youth. With blonde hair, a slim waist and blue eyes, he could have any girl he wanted.

He reckoned, with the right training, he could turn his hand to any seagoing job, from ordinary seaman to captain when experienced enough. Sailors he knew said that he might have to take a turn in the barrel. The reason for this, or what it entailed, the sailors had not explained to him, but he would not willingly participate in any abhorrent or depraved act, whatever it was.

The free spirit of youth speeded him to Liverpool and the River Mersey. Many beautiful, square-rigged ships traded from there. He was sure he could find employment. On arrival in the city, he walked the length of Dock Road. He saw drunken sailors and women of loose morals on the street. There were many vessels tied up on the river. He inspected them all on his perambulation, but he had no knowledge to help him with a choice of vessel on which to seek employment.

Raleigh chose the largest schooner he saw, the Mary Jane. Employment on board her might be easier, he guessed: it would have more crew than smaller vessels. Walking up the gangway to the deck, he marvelled at the beauty of the schooner. He thought Mary Jane must look a wonderful sight, fully rigged, under full sail.

Raleigh found the captain's cabin underneath the poop deck. He knocked and waited. A large red-faced man with whiskers and bushy sideburns, wearing long johns and a vest, opened the door to him and said gruffly, 'Yes.'

'Captain, I'm looking for employment at sea,' Raleigh said. I'd like to work on this ship in any capacity.'

'What seagoing experience do you have, young-un?' the captain asked.

'I don't have any, but I'm honest,' Raleigh said.

'Well, this might be your lucky day, young-un. I'm a hand short. You can start immediately at a shilling a week. I sail on the afternoon tide. Go below and see the bosun. He will train you up; see what stuff you're made of.'

Raleigh found life at sea harsh, hardtack every day, but he never thought it would be easy. The bosun wasn't hard on him and he learned to splice and repair ropes and to climb up the masts to unfurl the sails and check the rigging. No crewmate had yet mentioned the barrel. He had looked in the various cubbyholes where the bosun might have stowed the barrel. Not finding one in his first 5 days into the voyage, he put the tale down to fiction: sailor's tales for the landlubber to digest.

The Atlantic weather had been calm for the 5 days. A week out, a wind got up that had sails flapping. Within hours, the storm was tossing the Mary Jane about, burying her bow in foam-topped waves. The captain ordered the lowering of some sails.

Swabbing the decks with a brush was an onerous task that hadn't lit up Raleigh's heart as an important and necessary part of sailor's duties. Waves were washing the decks and he didn't see much sense in the task the bosun had set him. Perhaps it was only a pisstake the first tripper to fall for, but nobody had mentioned the barrel.

Sadly, a larger wave swept down the deck, lifted Raleigh off his feet. His size and strength couldn't save him, the wave crashing him over the rail into the oggin. The bosun rushed to see the captain and said to him, 'You know that lad you took on in Liverpool that said he was honest. I never got a chance to mention the barrel to him. Now, he's just pissed off over the rail and taken your brush with him!'

SCOUSE MEETS A GENIE

Scouse was a lifelong Liverpool FC supporter. He watched his first game at the age of five, sitting on his dad's shoulders in Anfield's Kop end, in the days when Kenny Dalglish and Peter Beardsley were in their pomp.

Scouse was taking his mongrel out for a walk, late one night, behind the Liver Building, adjacent the Pierhead. Suddenly, a genie appeared in front of Scouse. Seeing the quaintly attired individual stopped him in his tracks.

'Scouse, I can give you one wish,' said the genie, 'what will it be?'

Scouse said, 'Wow, a dream come true. I find it very embarrassing. It makes me the laughing stock of the Kop End on Saturdays when there's a game on. I'd like my dog to be quickly rid his phobia for all things Everton and their colour blue. He will only answer to me when I shout Ferguson. That's his name now and, around here, I've to be careful who hears me say it.

'I cannot get him out of the house without it wearing a blue coat, blue collar, blue bootees and blue lead or me with a pocket filled with toffees. He loves toffees. I have to feed the sweets secretly to him. I couldn't stand my mates seeing me doing it. He has only one leg the correct length. He's totally lopsided. He has half a tail. He has no ears and is cross-eyed, all from fighting. He has one testicle missing. A mad beagle bitch savaged and chewed it off during a fight.

'I would like Ferguson to learn to abhor his name and the colour blue. If you could see your way to correct some of his physical defects, have his

144

missing items replaced and him titivated up so I can enter him in Crufts dog show, it would be a bonus.'

The genie said, 'You're asking too much. I cannot work such miracles. Make another wish.' I'm not Sir Alex Ferguson.

'Can you ensure Liverpool players won't receive a yellow card for committing dangerous tackles and diving during any game this season?' Scouse asked.

The genie replied, 'I think I'd better take another look at the dog.'

BULLSHITTING SCOTTISH WIMMEN

It is twenty-five years since school friends Sophia, Olivia and Ella had seen each other, each going their separate ways since high school. They rediscover each other via a reunion website and arrange to meet for lunch at a Glasgow wine bar.

Sophia arrived first, wearing a Versace number in eggshell blue, her hair in a short, auburn bob. She ordered a bottle of Chardonnay, three glasses, and sat, looking out a window for her friends' arrival, taking an occasional sip of the wine.

Olivia arrived shortly afterward, wearing a daring outfit by Chanel, her blonde hair layered with bangs. After the required ritualised kisses, she joined Sophia and accepted a glass of wine.

Ella ambled in, wearing a faded Sex Pistols T-shirt, blue jeans and Wellington boots, her hair an elfin cut. She refused a glass of wine, and said she'd rather have a Guinness.

Sophia explains that after leaving high school and graduating from Glasgow University in Classics, she met and married Jonathan, with whom she has a beautiful daughter, Rebecca, now modelling, sought after for photo shoots worldwide, her photo often in the best magazines. Their other equally beautiful daughter Susanna attends The Royal Conservatoire of Scotland studying for a B.A in Dramatic Art. Jonathan is a partner in one of Glasgow's leading law firms. They live in a 4000 sq ft penthouse in Milngavie; they have a second home in Oban, on the seafront, overlooking The Sound of Kerrera.

Olivia, who is eager to relate her life matters since school, exudes that she graduated from The

University of Edinburgh with a degree in medicine and later qualified as a surgeon. She now commutes twice weekly from Perth to Edinburgh's Western General, where she works mainly with cancer patients. Her husband Clive is a leading Perth investment banker. They live in Kinfauns and have a second home in Pitlochry. On holiday there, they often see a member of the royal family walk past their home without security in tow.

Ella explains that she left school at 16 and ran off with her boyfriend Jock. They both joined the Army and served together in Afghanistan. They now run a hunting business near Tomintoul. Snow blocks them in most winters, for weeks on end, where they live, making it difficult to leave their dilapidated bothy, high in the Cairngorm hills. They grow their own vegetables and eat rabbit or grouse, occasionally venison. They have a still and make their own hooch. Jim can hang seven ferrets, by their front claws, side by side, on his erect penis.

Halfway down a fourth bottle of Buckfast and several hours later, Sophia blurts out that her husband is really a cashier in a Govan Pound Shop. They live in a council tower block in Paisley and haven't had a holiday in years.

Olivia, chastened and encouraged by her old friend's honesty, explains that she and Clive are both pisspot emptiers in a Granton retirement home. They live in a Leith tower block and take an annual day excursion by bus to Glasgow, to see her brother-in-law in Barlinnie, doing life.

Ella explained that one ferret has to hang on by one leg.

BULLSHITTING AUSSIE WIMMEN

Jan, Sue and Sheila had not seen each other since high school. They rediscover each other via a reunion website and arrange to meet for lunch at a Sydney wine bar.

Jan arrived first, wearing a Versace number in beige. She ordered a bottle of Pinot Grigio and sat sipping it.

Sue arrived shortly afterward, wearing a daring outfit by Chanel. After the required ritualised kisses, she joined Jan and accepted a glass of Pinot.

Sheila ambled in, wearing a faded old T-shirt, blue jeans and Outback boots. She too accepted a glass of Pinot, and said she'd rather have a Fosters.

Jan explains that after leaving high school and graduating from Sydney University in Classics, she met and married Timothy, with whom she has a beautiful daughter.

Timothy is a partner in one of Sydney's leading law firms. They live in a 4000 sq ft penthouse at Darling Point, while Susanna, the daughter, attends drama school. They have a second home in Port Douglas.

Sue relates that she graduated from Sydney Med School and became a surgeon. Her husband, Clive, is a leading Sydney investment banker. They live in Point Piper and have a second home in Noosa.

Sheila explains that she left school at 17 and ran off with her boyfriend, Jim. They run a tropical bird park in Queensland and grow their own vegetables. Jim can stand five parrots, side by side, on his erect penis.

Halfway down the third bottle of wine and several hours later, Jan blurts out that her husband is really a cashier at Target. They live in a small apartment in Asquith and have a trailer parked at a nearby storage facility.

Sue, chastened and encouraged by her old friend's honesty, explains that she and Clive are both pisspot emptiers in a retirement home. They live in Blacktown and vacation taking camping trips to Woy Woy.

Sheila explained that a parrot has to stand on one leg.

ELECTRONIC DDT REPLACEMENT

The new plug in electronic fly repellent device Flugermax hits the market today. Plagued householders can now get rid of their homemade cayenne pepper, peppermint lemongrass, eucalyptus, camphor and cinnamon sprays that have little effect on the annoying pests. No longer will the fly plagued need to burn citronella candles or hang up plastic bags of water with a handful of copper pennies in the bottom. The vinegar flytrap becomes redundant as well as those antifly and insect killing products recommended by pest experts and expensive to repeatedly purchase from supermarkets.

Householder can personalize the Flugermax to their choice of daily newspaper. The device emits the whisper of a rolled up newspaper scything through the air. You can program from the reverberation an unwieldy Daily Times makes to that of a lightweight red top like the Daily Sport, as they reach Mach1 on their flight path to the target.

Manufacturer Flugerarmextend expect Flugermax orders to fly off the shelf.

RETIREMENT HOME BRIEFING

Barlanark born porn star of fifty years, with the topmost male position in seven hundred and fifty feature length films, performing name, Tadger Hungwell, retired from the porno movie business. His family put him in the care of an Edinburgh nursing home.

On their first visit to the home, family members were keen to know if Tadger was happy living in care.

Tadger explained, 'The staff members here treat everyone with respect. That man over there, looking through the window up to the sky, Captain Biggles, was a pilot in his working life with BA. He daily gives patients and staff member's in-depth lectures on the various aircraft he flew, and how to fly them successfully and safely into every airport in the world to where BA flies. I believe many staff members have learned so much from him that they have obtained their pilot's licence. Staff members address him as captain.

'That elderly man sitting in the armchair reading the medical journal, Doctor Butcher, was a battlefield medic in the Bosnian war and an Army surgeon. Doctor Butcher gives daily lectures on all things medical. Most staff members are crack first aiders. Some staff members have left to enrol at university to study for a medical degree. Present staff members address him as Doctor.

Staff members also treat me with the utmost respect, taking into account my profession; they address me as That Fucking Glaswegian.

TIMOTHY'S QUANDARY

Timothy hadn't realised the many ways that his wife Maisie's pregnancy would affect him. Old wives' tales suggested that pregnant women went through a fondness phase for unusual foodstuffs. Eating raw onions was high on that list of foods appealing to the pregnant. Maisie must have known that she could suffer this fondness for strange foods. With prior knowledge or not, she started tucking into onions, raw, pickled or fried and pickled eggs.

Timothy found the smell it left on Maisie's breath nauseating.

Also on the old wifies' tale list was a suggestion that pregnancy-symptoms sharing could affect the father of the expected child; weight gain, altered hormone levels, morning sickness and disturbed sleep patterns amongst them, The medical world know the sympathetic pregnancy as the 'couvade syndrome'.

Timothy felt that to prove his love for Maisie he had to fall into line; sod waiting for the wifie's tales to kick in: start eating the same foods she fancied.

That worked when he was alone in his wife's company. Work colleagues were standing back from him; some saying his breath was rotten, when he spoke to them.

Timothy reckoned that if he told his fellow workers or anyone in the village how he was mimicking Maisie's food fancies, some of them would hold him up to ridicule, be the butt of every joke, be the laughing stock. The whole pregnancy thing was getting on top of him.

And he couldn't get on top of his wife for sex. The bump was in the way and so was the 'Not on your fucking Nellie' retort form Maisie whenever he moved too close to her in bed.

Maisie's lack of sexual urges was the pregnancy manifestation that troubled him most.

Masturbation was Timothy's last resort, his only outlet. He succumbed to the practice that he'd given up on marriage or unless Maisie took him in hand. He began to enjoy the experience again, having a quick one over the wrist whenever, without recourse to coarse thought, or looking at sexy photos of half-naked women in magazines.

Timothy didn't need any impulse to fancy a wank.

He found to his surprise that he was having a quick one whilst attending his annual eye test at the local opticians. The optician approached him and said, 'You will have to stop wanking.'

Timothy looked away from his jerking hand and asked the optician, 'Will it have an effect on my eyesight?'

'No,' the optician said, with a look of annoyance on his serious face, 'you're upsetting my other customers!'

GIFT WRAPPED IN LEEDS

Noddy wanted to buy a pressie for his new bird, Chloe. They'd been going out for a week and he wanted to impress and surprise her.

After giving it thought, he decided that a pair of mittens would please her, were not a starry-eyed gift and not too special.

Accompanied by his sister, he went to Poundstretcher in Leeds and bought a pair of white mittens. His sister purchased a pair of knickers for herself.

During the packaging, the shop assistant mixed up the two items. Noddy's sister had the mittens, Chloe the knickers!

Without checking the contents, Noddy printed on the package SWALK and posted it to his bird with the following note:

Dear Chloe,

I chose these because I noticed that you are not in the habit of wearing any when we go out. If it had not been for my sister, I would have chosen the long ones with the buttons, but she wears short ones that are easier to remove. These are a delicate shade, but the shop assistant showed me the pair that she had been wearing for the past three weeks, which she hadn't soiled at all.

I had her try yours on for me and she looked spectacular, even though she stretched them a bit. She also told me that her pair helps to keep her ring clean and shiny; indeed, she had not needed to rinse them through since she first put them on.

I wish I could be with you to help put them on for the first time. No doubt, many other hands will touch them before I have a chance to see you again.

When you take them off, remember to blow into them before putting them away: they will naturally be a little moist from wearing.

Just think how many times kisses will land on them during the coming year.

I hope that you will take them off for me on Friday night and let me hold what's in them.

Looking forward to seeing you,

Noddy

P.S. The latest style is to wear them folded down with a little fur showing.

HOSS FLIES

Eugene and Larry were friends since boyhood. They regularly questioned each other over their knowledge of the entomology of the flies flitting about in a dizzying fashion over the New Orleans township of Gretna, where they both had lived since birth. Neither of the New Orleanians had an ology in anything

This particular Gretna lies on the banks of the Mississippi River. They had never heard of the famous one that lies near the banks of the River Sark, on the border of Scotland and England. Great swarms of flies, congregating on Mississippi's banks, look for a dead animal, human being or a nourishing turd to float by, then wing out across the swirling water in a black cloud to descend on whatever floats there, for a good tuck in.

It was in the heat of the day that Eugene and Larry were walking, side-by-side, down Gretna's main drag. There were flies everywhere. Stray dogs and horses left behind them on the streets vast piles of, succulent to the fly, shit.

Eugene said to Larry, 'Hey, Larry, what's those hoss flies doing flittin' about your face?'

Larry replied, 'Goddone it, Eugene, how you know these is hoss flies?

'Well, Larry,' Eugene said, 'they's one of those type of flies you see flittin' around a hosses ass, mostly when the weather is scorching and the hosses tail is going mental trying to flap away the annoying critters.'

'Now come on, Eugene,' said Larry, 'you is suggesting ma face has the appearance of a hosses ass?'

'Well, no,' Larry, 'but you sure got those flies confused!'

MY THOUGHTS ON THE HAGGIS

I've tried, in the past, to debunk the laughable, media-created fiction circulating news channels regarding this incredible, non-extinct animal indigenous to Scotland.

To ensure the species survival, I will strongly campaign for a dedicated winter habitat, free of predators, with adequate shelter on slopes not too steep, which provide a staple food source: natural white heather their favourite bite.

The Haggis's well-trodden, annual migration routes to southerly, lower level, summer feeding grounds, dawn-of-time Old Caledonia ordinance survey maps clearly define. I'd have underpasses created beneath byways, highways, major roads and motorways, thus ensuring the beasts' safer passage as they scurry hurriedly, from their winter uplands, each year, to reach their summer pastures by the June solstice.

I worked down the Falklands from November 1982 to February 1983, looking after a ferry taken up from trade, a (STUFT) ship, during the war there. Years later, a friend invited me to submit photographs to a Falklands photographic site. I had several photos of the islands as they looked after the destruction of the war. I put this photograph up with a spoof story that it was a shot of the last known Falklands Haggis, it having fallen into a valley beneath Mount Tumbledown and had died there, in a deep gulley.

Photographic site wardens threw me off the site. Obviously, humourless Islanders, known to the forces that saved them from the Argentineans as Bennies, because they tended to wear the same shaped bonnet that Benny from of the TV soap Crossroads, had never heard of the Falkland's Haggis. How ignorant of the fauna of the islands is that?

I wondered if we could we create an annual festival, entitled The Adoration of the Haggii, situated somewhere on the Kyles of Bute, the last known domicile of the beast on the Western Isles.

The inserted photograph is the only existing image of a Haggis. This is a male, proved, at the time of its demise, by testicular examination by an experienced chicken sexer, possibly of Chinese origins.

The snapper took the shot using an early camera, the image fixed onto a glass plate coated with silver chloride, which darkened when exposed to light. The photograph shows the beast happily grazing bluebells near a hedge in its summer pastures, a rare sighting of this predominately, heather eating, hillside dweller.

Its front, telescopic legs are an evolutionary wonder, unknown in any other species, worldwide, alive or extinct. Nature had decreed the need for telescopic front pins: without them, the species would become extinct, the result of unsteadiness on narrow trails situated high on the slopes, their well-documented course-reversal abilities being fraught with danger.

CHRISTMAS DINNER

Picture the scene: It is Christmas Day in the Schultz family home.

Adolph Schultz is a proud man. He has made his fortune developing pharmaceuticals to alleviate hunger: to suppress the appetites of overeating Americans. Americans tote the largest bellies in the entire world. How could he lose?

Adolph's three sons, all in different years at Yale, had arrived home for the celebrations in the Limo he had hired, together with a chauffeur, to pick them up on campus. Adolph was aghast when he saw them, when he rightly should have been pleased to see all three. That morning of Christmas day, he had brooded while he watched the level in the bourbon bottle sitting next to his glass slip down to its floor.

Earlier, the family cook had managed to negotiate the thirty-pound turkey stuffed with a sage, onion and chestnut stuffing into the Aga, at gas mark 4 for 7 hours. Adolph mused, squeezing a bird that big into the oven the cook had carried out in a Houdini-like fashion. It would feed a whole tribe of Africans, not a family of five. He had seen the gargantuan size two of his sons had reached whilst at Yale. Now he wondered if he should have ordered another bird.

Dinner was served at 3pm. Adolph sat at one end of the oblong mahogany table, Dolores, his wife, sat opposite him. Gregory and Thomas sat at one side of the table, whilst Horace sat alone on the other side.

The menu was spectacular: pate de foie gras on sourdough toast for the entree, Turkey with trimmings the main course. Mississippi mud pie and ice cream for sweet.

Before the maid served coffee, Adolph rose slowly to his feet. He was a big man, with a generous overhang that his tailor had concealed, to the best of his ability, within loose fitting trousers. Adolph was florid of complexion and sweat coursed from his brow as he looked at each of his boys in turn. In his earlier musing, he decided he had to give Horace and Gregory a piece of his mind, Thomas words of wonder and congratulation.

'Horace, son,' Adolph began his rant, 'look at you. 'You're 22 and what weight are you now. About 230 Kilos, is my guess. You're nothing but a fat, overfed bastard. How the hell have you managed to put that much dripping on in your short life? What the fuck are they feeding you at Yale?'

Horace, looking horrified at his father, responded, 'I only eat what the rest of class and the family eat, I just take big bites.'

'You'll have to learn to take smaller bites,' Adolph said.

He looked at Gregory and said, 'What's your excuse? You're only, 20 yet you must be 160 kilos, already. You're well on your way to being a huge and overweight bastard, like Horace, when you reach his age.'

'I only eat the same as Horace and the family,' moaned Gregory, 'and like Horace, I take big bites.'

'You, too, will have to learn to take smaller bites,' Adolph said.

He looked at Thomas and asked, 'You're 19 now. How the fuck have you stayed so skinny? You're as thin as a telegraph pole.'

Thomas responded, 'I only eat pussy,'

'You only eat pussy, Adolph erupted, spittle flying from his lips. That tastes like shit!'

'Dad, you will have to learn to take smaller bites,' Thomas said.

HECHOS GORDOS (FAT FACTS)

I feel sorry for the obesidad morbida (morbidly obese), I do, especially the poor senor from Madrid. This particular food-lover had gorged himself up to 476.272 Kg (75 stone), putting away ten burgers, ten portions of KF chicken, two dozen eggs, thirty-five tapas, twelve portions of toast with garlic and olive oil, a kilo of Albran and a litre of sangria for his desayuno (breakfast).

Doctoras (Doctors) ordered his immediate hospitalisation. Apart from his colossal size, he was suffering from arthritis, high cholesterol and blood sugar levels, and sleep apnea. He was in acute danger of having a stroke or a heart attack. The least of his problems was disfuncion erectil (erectile dysfunction): he couldn't find his pene (penis).

Doctors requested Bomberos (Firemen) break into his casa (home) last week. Further health complications, (constipacion cronica) chronic constipation, necessitated his extraction. Andamios (Scaffolders) and expertasen demolicion (demolition experts) took the front out of his casa. Aparejadoras, (Riggers) using chain blocks and slings dragged him onto a pallet. A forklift truck took him the viaje (journey). Five bomberos are on permanent duty in the ward for his first mierda (shit). Two to roll him in flour so they can find the crack in his culo (arse), two to hold the cheeks apart and one to hose him down when he's finished.

Aqui termina la leccion de espanol. (Here endeth the Spanish lesson).

164

SAVE THE EFFLUENT

To preserve a disappearing species from our planet, you can now adopt an Effluent. The adoption does not come free. It will not only cost you a monthly fee, you will also have to factor in the cost of dedication to ensure no plastics remain concealed in the nourishment this beast will require throughout its long life. The Effluent abhors alien foodstuff blockages. You will also have to remember that the Effluent never forgets. It could come rushing back at the most inopportune moment and overwhelm you. Many adoptees have recorded gaseous, gory experiences. It can be an unforgiving beast.

The Effluent is easily recognisable: it has a round, tank-like shape with a hose protruding from its leading end for feeding in nutrients and an earth enrichment release and wafting mechanism at the extreme end of the tank.

For an insignificant £3 a month, you can legally adopt an Effluent, preserve, nurture and prolong the life of the species, ensuring the Effluent has the daily, prescribed flush of nourishment.

Apply now to The Effluent Adoption Society.

ANAL REVELATION

Gladys had recently become a widow. Her husband Richard had died suddenly at home, a cerebral infarction, the attending doctor had said. The undertaker had already paid her a home visit to finalise funeral arrangements. Gladys did not expect to receive a telephone call from the chapel of rest.

The undertaker said when he called, 'I've run into a problem with the laying out and burial of your husband. Richard has developed a huge and outrageously stiff erection. I will not be able to get the lid onto the coffin and close it properly.'

The widow asked, 'Can you not drill a hole in the coffin lid and shove it through, then cut off the head. It will look like a knot in the wood and nobody attending the funeral will notice.'

The undertaker said, 'That wouldn't look right. All my coffins are knot free and I will not change my standards or risk my good name. The top has to look perfect.'

The widow asked, 'What do you suggest?'

The undertaker replied, 'In other cases, we've simply sliced off the erection at its base, then slipped it into the anus, out of the way, out of sight, out of mind, no embarrassment, no one will know its final destination.'

The widow replied, 'If that's what you have to do, then I agree. Go ahead and perform the penectomy or whatever the technical term is.'

That afternoon, Gladys visited the chapel of rest to view her husband laid out. Gladys thought Richard looked refined dressed in his Sunday best. Then she noticed a tear trickling down from one of his closed eyes. Gladys leaned over the coffin and whispered into his ear, 'I told you it was fucking painful!'

SHORTS

Went for my routine check up today and everything seemed to be going fine until he stuck his index finger up my arse!

Do you think I should change dentists?

My wife was married three times before bagging me. Her first husband was a gynaecologist who didn't want sex. He only wanted to look at it. Her second was a psychologist who didn't want sex. He only wanted to talk to it. Her third was a stamp collector. She really misses him.

Being old, the plumber's position is mandatory for us. It's in all day, but no one comes.

The first time I took my wife to a restaurant, I asked her if she liked scampi. She said she liked all Walt Disney films.

A wife was frying eggs for her husband's breakfast. Suddenly, her husband burst into the kitchen. 'Careful,' he said, 'be fucking careful. Put some more oil in the frying pan. Oh my gosh, you're cooking too many at once. Turn them now. I don't want sunny-side up. We need more oil. Oh dear, are you going to put in more oil. They're going to stick to the pan. Careful, it's not non-stick. I said be careful. You never listen to me when you're cooking. Never. Turn the bloody eggs, won't you. Hurry up. Are you crazy? Have you lost your mind? Don't forget to salt them.

You know you always forget to salt them. Use the Salt. The salt.'

His wife stared at him. 'What in the world is wrong with you? You think I don't know how to fry eggs?'

The husband calmly replied, 'I just want you to know what it feels like when I'm driving with you as a back seat driver.'

SHEILA'S TWELVE DAYS OF AUSSIE CHRISTMAS.

December 14th
My dearest darling Bruce:
Whoever in the whole world would dream of receiving a Sulphur-crested Cockatoo in a coolabah tree? How can I ever express my pleasure? Thank you a hundred times for thinking of me this way. It was fair dinkum. You are such a nice person.
My love always.
Sheila

December 15th
Dearest Bruce:
Today, the postie brought me your very sweet gift of two beautiful Magpie Larks. I'm just delighted at your very thoughtful gift. They have a nice, unforgettable tweet. They are just adorable.
All my love.
Sheila

December 16
Dear Bruce:
Oh! Aren't you the extravagant one? Now I must protest. I don't deserve such generosity: three Quail Thrushes that are just darling and cute, have a raucous threnody to their call. However, I must insist, you've been too kind.
All my love.
Sheila

December 17th
Dear Bruce:
Today the postie delivered four Barking Owls. They haven't stopped making doggie sounds. All the dogs in the neighbourhood are at my garden gate sniffing, showing their lipstick, trying to clamber over. I think these owls are bitches and barking mad. They are beautiful. However, don't you think enough is enough? You are becoming quite a romantic.
Affectionately yours
Sheila

December 18th
Dearest Bruce:
What a surprise. Today the postie delivered five golden rings. There's one for each finger of one hand, but oh are they big. I'll have to use them for putting up a high decibel sound-deadening curtain between my bedroom and the rest of the house. All the squawking and quarrelling is getting on my nerves a bit.
 Frankly, all the birds you've sent me are lovely. I've had a construction firm quickly build an aviary onto the bungalow as it is becoming too small to house them all.
You're just impossible, but I love the attention.
All my love
Sheila

December 19th
Dear Bruce:
When I opened the door to the postie today, there were six Magpie Geese, fully grown, laying on my

front steps. So you're back to the birds lark again. Excuse my pun!

These geese are huge. Where will I ever keep them? The neighbours are complaining about the honking and the racket my other feathered friends are making. Your gifts are kicking up various loud noises, ranging from a screech to a riverboat horn, or is it whistle? I'm becoming confused. I wish I were deaf. I can't sleep through the confounded noise. That curtain is going up to cover my bedroom door.

Please stop before you piss me off, for good.

Sheila

December 20th

Bruce:

What's with you and the fucking birds thing? Seven fucking Laughing Kookaburras; what kind of dumb fucking joke is this? I think the Kooks are telling jokes in turn and the other birds are screeching their fucking heads off, nearly falling off their roosts. There's bird shit all over the house. The honks the tweets and the trills the barks never fucking stop. I can't sleep at night. I haven't found an acoustic product retailer. I'm a nervous wreck. It's not funny. Don't send any more fucking birds!

I mean it.

Sheila

December 21st

O.K. Buster:

I think I prefer the birds. What, in God's name, am I going to do with eight flimsily-dressed Cowgirls a milking? The gift of all those birds was vastly over the fucking top. Now I've eight fucking unruly Texan

wimmen a milking and they've brought their fucking Jackasses, or are they mules, unruly bloody beasts, with them. There is horseshit all over the lawn, great dollops of it, piled high, and I can't move in my own house for bird droppings. Give my head some fucking peace, smartass.
Sheila

December 22nd
Hey Shithead:
Are you some kind of sadist? Now I've nine poorly dressed Didgeridoo players with no arse in their jeans with all the sitting they've been doing. Fuck me, do they play some awful tunes; the fucking geese are trying to match the sound with their honking. It's a diabolical fucking chorus. Believe me. When the Didgers stop playing, they all dig into a pocket and fetch out a pack of bush tucker: dried witchety grubs. The birds all go fucking crazy when they sight them and aren't offered any. The Didgers haven't stopped chasing the Cowgirls since they got here yesterday morning. Milking the men of all of their seminal juices, that's all the milking the Cowgirls have been doing. The asses are upset; they barged indoors and shit all over those screeching birds. What am I going to do? The neighbours have started a petition to evict me. Environmental Health Johnnies have been here and rigged up noise detectors everywhere. They talk of annoying decibels. I'm in deep shit in more ways than one. You're getting to be an inconsiderate piece of shit.
You'll get your feathers plucked when I catch up with you, bastard!
Sheila

December 23rd

You rotten prick:

Now the latest gift to arrive is ten Gins dancing. I cannot call the Gins ladies; they've been balling the Didgeridoo players all night long. Now the asses can't sleep and have diarrhoea, my lawn grass looks brown, not a patch of greenery anywhere, looks like summer has come early. My living room is a river running high with bird shit. The Commissioner of Buildings has summoned me to give cause as to why he should not condemn the building.

I'm calling the cops to sort you out, you fucking retard!

Sheila

December 24th

Listen Fuckwit:

What's with these eleven Drongos leaping delivered today? In what outback hellhole did you find them? Those Texan bitches are fucking Cowpokes; the Drongos haven't given them or the Gins peace since they arrived. Leaping, they've buried the sausage several times over, the perverts. Some of the women have gone bandy and will never walk properly again. Those didgeridoo players have done the business with the Gins and committed sodomy with the asses. The asses seemed to have liked it, trying to turn round to kiss a having a shag Drongo whilst he's on the job, hanging on to the tail to retain connection. All twenty-three of the birds are dead, trampled to death in the orgy. I hope you're satisfied, you rotten, vicious swine. Have you a kangaroo running amok in the top paddock. I hope a funnel web spider bites your arse, and a taipan spews its venom into your bollocks, all at the same time, bastard.

Sheila

December 25th
Dear Sir:
This is to acknowledge your latest gift of twelve ukulele players strumming, which you have seen fit to inflict on our client, Miss Sheila Brucellosis. With the other gifts, her destruction, of course, was total. We will redirect all correspondence to Miss Brucellosis. We have instructed the attendants at Woolloomooloo Sanatorium to shoot you on sight if you attempt to make contact with her. With this letter, please find attached a photocopy of the warrant for your arrest. Our advice: give yourself up to the nearest police station.
Cordially,
Law Offices of Roger, Bender & Hole.

EASY LINERS

My new girlfriend told me was married three times before bagging me. Her first husband was a gynaecologist who didn't want sex. He only wanted to look at it. Her second was a psychologist who didn't want sex. He only wanted to talk to it. Her third was a stamp collector. She really misses him.

I told her I was suffering from piles. She said, 'You shouldn't be sitting on that beanbag.'
    I replied, 'I'm not sitting on a beanbag!

Last night I was sitting on the sofa watching TV. I heard my girlfriend's voice from the kitchen, 'What you like for dinner my love, chicken, beef or lamb?'
    I said, 'Thank you, I'll have chicken please.'
    She replied, 'You're having soup you fat bastard, I was talking to the cat!'

I first met Lenny in the Dumpy Bar in Fuengirola. He was a bar fly most nights that I popped in for a pint or two of San Miguel. He told me he rented a studio apartment in a local block every year for six months. I had met him in the bar each year of my five consecutive annual holidays spent there. He was a happy-go-lucky Geordie with a good line of patter, mainly about football and his favourite team, Newcastle United and their great players down the years.
    Then he disappeared. None of the bar staff knew why. Guesses ranged from he'd gone home, had died, had found another holiday destination. No one I spoke to was sure.

Ten years later, I was retired and owned an apartment there. I was spending many winters on the Costa del Sol.

To my surprise, Lenny reappeared. He'd been missing for some time. He looked as if he had just flown in, his skin milk-bottle white. He was sitting towards the back of the pub, out of the sunlight. I was eager to have a chat with him, to find out if all was well in his life.

At first, Lenny wouldn't be drawn on giving a reason for his absence, was quite reticent to open up, but I persisted with my questioning until he blurted, 'I've just finished a ten year sentence in Malaga jail.'

'What for?' was my immediate question.

'You'll keep on asking until I tell you so I might as well get it over with,' he said. 'I was in for bestiality. I was caught shafting a Dalmatian.'

'How the fuck did that happen?' I asked. I'm sure I looked as shocked as anyone else would be on hearing such an admission.

'That night, I was totally pissed, ratarsed. I thought I was laying a domino,' he answered.

I didn't spot that one coming!

I never married her: I reckoned I might have had six happy months of marriage out of the 46 years.

A biker tells his doctor of hearing problems. 'Describe the symptoms?' The doctor asked. 'Homer is a fat yellow lazy bastard and Marge is a skinny bird with big blue hair.'

ANGUS IN AMBERLAND

Angus was going on a cruise. As soon as his daughter Trixie heard the news, she was on the phone to him, 'Dad, dad,' she said excitedly, 'are you going to fetch me something nice home from the cruise?'

'What nice would you want me to fetch you back from the cruise. Would you want something you think nice or something I think nice?' Angus asked.

'Oh, something you think nice,' Trixie said.

'Would you consider an empty Viagra box something I think nice?' Angus asked.

'Enjoy the cruise, Dad, I was only teasing,' Trixie said, knowing her dad was only teasing her.

The cruise liner left the port of Southampton, headed east along the English Channel, then north up the North Sea. It took the short cut to the Baltic sea through the Kiel Canal, a slower, but shorter, and a more scenic route, to arrive in the Estonian capital city of Tallinn after a 4-day voyage.

Walking around Tallinn, Angus spotted a small jewellery shop. Perhaps, in there, he thought, he would find a small frippery denoting a particular aspect of Estonian history or culture that Trixie might like.

It was clear to Angus as soon as he had entered the shop that the availability of a frippery that included a slab of amber was a distinct possibility. He browsed several display cabinets, a girl assistant constantly by his side, eager to advise and obtain a sale.

Angus spotted a shiny piece of amber on a silver mounting, with a clasp that indicated Trixie could wear it as a broach.

'How much is this piece?' He asked the hovering assistant.

'That piece is two hundred and fifty Euros,' the girl informed him, in heavily accented English.

Shocked at what he thought an exorbitant price, Angus asked, 'Why is it so expensive?'

'Because it has a fly encapsulated in the amber,' the girl replied.

Forever the wise-cracker, Angus asked, 'Is there also room in the amber for the zip?'

Scottish parsimony setting in, Angus thought the cost much more than he intended to spend on a frippery for Trixie. The Viagra box remained unopened, which hadn't improved his humour. He thought of a postcard to send from the port and asked the girl, 'Do you keep stationery?

'I do when I start,' the girl said, 'but when I finish I'm going like a bunny rabbit!'

MORE LINERS

Coppers nicked Rocky for wife beating. The judge said to Rocky, 'You've been up in front of me before for this offence. Why do you keep beating her?'

Rocky answered, 'I think it's my weight advantage, longer reach, superior foot work and her glass chin.'

Age destroys the memory, that's for sure. This morning I went upstairs. Half way up the stairs, I forgot why I was going up the stairs. I went back down the stairs to try to figure out why I was going up the stairs. That's when I shit myself!

I arrived home from the pub in the early hours. Snowflakes were falling thickly. I built a snow woman. She was beautiful, white and perfect. I thought I'd keep her as a pet. I let her sleep with me. I made her some pyjamas and a pillow for her head. This morning she had vanished and left me alone in a pissed bed.

Dear Sir, on behalf of the Gut Reduction TV Channel, I thank you for submitting an application on behalf of your girlfriend, to take part in our new reality show, and the charming photograph of her you enclosed. Whilst agreeing she would make a worthy contribution to the program. If selected, I would point out that the correct title of the series is actually 'fact hunt'.

Billy took two stuffed dogs to the Antiques Roadshow for expert appraisal.

'Ooh!' the expert said, 'this is a very rare example of an uncommon breed. Do you have any idea what they would fetch if they were in good condition?
'Sticks,' Billy replied

Hey, mate, just a quick one. I need your advice. Instead of buying a turkey for Christmas dinner this year, I've been offered 8 legs of venison for £40. Do you think that's two deer?'

Brenda was at home making dinner for husband Sean, when his best friend Tim knocked on her door. 'Brenda, may I come in?' Tim asked, 'I've something important to tell you.'

Brenda replied, 'Of course you can come in. You're always welcome here. I was expecting Sean. Did he not walk home from work with you?'

'That's what I'm here to be telling you, Brenda. There was an accident at the brewery.'

'Oh, God no!' Brenda cried out, 'don't tell me Sean was involved.'

'I must tell you, Brenda. Sean is dead and gone. I'm sorry.' Tim said.

Brenda collapsed into an armchair, found a handkerchief in an apron pocket and began to sob into it. After a while, she looked up at Tim and asked, 'How did it happen?'

'It was terrible, Brenda. Sean fell into a vat of stout and drowned.'

'Oh my dear Jesus,' Brenda erupted, 'Tim, you must tell me truth, did he suffer.'

'Brenda, Sean definitely wasn't suffering at all. In fact, before he went, he got out three times to take a piddle.'

BOGGED DOWN

It was late on Saturday morning. Dougie was shopping in Glasgow's Buchannan Galleries. He'd eaten onion bhajis and a superheated chicken vindaloo carryout the night before, which he'd downed with relish whilst drinking cans of Guinness as a cooling agent.

On the train from East Kilbride to Central Station his stomach rumbled. It had not eased in the mall whilst window-shopping for a pair of working boots. He needed to go.

He took the escalator to the next floor. A sign told him of the toilets direction. Walking quickly, clenched of nether cheeks, he entered the Gents block. He noted a door swinging open signalling a blessed vacant cubicle. He entered the cubicle, looked to see the seat was down, turned, locked the door, didn't bother to read any graffiti on the door back, loosened his belt, lowered his trousers to his ankles, sat down on the pan, let it flow, felt the heat of the chilli on his ringpiece.

Whilst he prepared for the fetid, fiery passing to cease, his eyes and a hand wandered to the area of the wall where he believed he would find the toilet roll. There was the raised piece of wood, but no roll holder: nothing there to wipe his arse. He looked right and left behind him, on the cistern top, but saw no wiping material. Had he not started the passing of what turned out to be a loose stool, he thought he might have paused the moment, clenched his nether cheeks tighter, and gone looking for the some material; but he had been desperate, was unaware of the situation.

Dougie tapped his pockets to see if there might be a hanky or even a supermarket receipt he might use. Alas, he found nothing to use as a wipe.

With a feeling of relief, he heard someone enter the adjacent cubicle and settle onto the pan: help was at hand.

There was a space beneath the partition between the cubicles. He tapped on the wall, directed his voice down towards the gap and said, 'Would you have some spare toilet roll in there? Some bastard has stolen it from here. I've nothing to wipe with.'

'Naw, I cannae help you mate. There's only two pieces left on the roll here. I'll have to use the cardboard inner for my final scrape. You smell as if you've a problem, right enough,' the voice said.

'Have you got a newspaper?' Dougie asked.

'Aye,' the voice advised.

'Can you give me a sheet out of the paper, please,' Dougie asked.

'Naw,' the voice advised.

'Why not? I'll give you the money to buy another.'

'I cannae.'

'Why not?'

'It's lying on the back seat of my car in the multi-storey.'

'What about a sheet from a glossy magazine. I'll accept any help I can get.'

'I've one o' them.'

'Can you please let me have a sheet? I'll buy you another when I get out o' here.'

'I cannae.'

'Why not?'

'The wife has it in her shopping bag.'

183

'Fucking arsehole. You're having me on!'

In desperation, Dougie took his wallet from an inside pocket, opened it and took out a £10 note. He was desperate, but he had one last idea that might be a cheaper alternative. He hollered down to the gap, 'Hey you in there. Have you two fivers for a tenner?'

HUGO THE MESSAGE BOY

Felix was shopping for French ticklers in a chemist's when he first noticed the beagle scampering alongside him, with the handle of the bag it carried secure in its jaws. The dog had a collar, but no lead. It was unaccompanied. Dog and man approached the counter together. Just as Felix was about to put his weekend order to the counter woman, she said to the dog, 'It's you again Hugo. What is it you want this time?'

Felix was surprised at the familiarity the woman showed to the dog. He reeled, when Hugo dropped the bag it was carrying, cocked a leg against a stand displaying dental products, splashed a drop of urine against it, then began to pant noisily.

The counter woman, having read the charade correctly, said, 'Ah, incontinent pants. Are they for mummy?'

Astounded, Felix watched Hugo nod his head in reply.

The woman walked from behind the counter to a display stacked with female protection garments, chose a packet and walked back behind the counter with it. 'Is that everything today, Hugo?' the woman asked.

Hugo reared on his back legs and placed his paws onto the counter front. Amazed, Felix watched the redness of Hugo's penis tip slowly emerge from its furry sheath.

Felix knew that the counter woman played charades and often read the clues accurately when she said, 'Ah, lipstick.' The woman left the counter for the display offering a multitude of female beauty enhancers. There she chose the particular shade that mummy must have bought before. She placed the purchases into the bag and placed the handle into Hugo's jaws. Then she opened the purse attached to Hugo's collar, removed a £20 note, registered the sale, placed the note in the till, then placed change into the purse.

Transfixed by the odd situation he had witnessed, Felix forgot about any weekend jollies his girlfriend had promised and followed Hugo from the store.

Next door to the chemist's a butcher traded. Hugo walked into the shop through the open door and sat down. Felix followed and stood next to Hugo. He was keen to see what transpired in that shop. The butcher, from behind the counter, said to the beagle, 'Ah, Hugo, What is it your after today?'

The Hugo lifted a paw and pointed it at a tray heaped with beef mince, on display behind the glass of the counter. The butcher said to Hugo, 'How much do you want?'

Hugo lifted a paw twice.

'Two pounds of beef mince,' the butcher said, then asked, 'anything else, Hugo?

Hugo shuffled along and lifted a paw to the glass. 'Ah, lamb chops,' said the butcher, 'how many?'

Hugo lifted a paw four times.

'Anything else?' The butcher asked.

Hugo turned around, lifted his tail, rotated it to one side, and showed the butcher his backside. 'A faggot,' the butcher said, then asked, 'is that it for today?

Hugo nodded his head in reply. The butcher wrapped up the order and placed it in a plastic bag.

Hugo walked behind the counter. The butcher opened the purse hanging from Hugo's collar, took out a ten-pound note, rang the price up, selected change from the till and placed it in the purse. The butcher then dropped the order into Hugo's bag. Loaded up, Hugo left the shop, the bag swinging.

Felix, eager to see who owned such a special dog, followed it out of the shop and along one-hundred yards of a pavement. Hugo entered through a gate to the front of a terraced house, clambered up two steps, raised a paw and began scratching at a lower door panel. Mummy opened the door and retrieved the bag from Hugo's jaws.

Felix said to mummy, 'What a wonderful, intelligent dog you have.'

Mummy replied, 'Hugo, he's fucking useless. That's twice this week he's forgotten his key. Yesterday, I sent him to the ironmongers for a long screw. He was humping the assistant's leg for so long, apparently enjoying himself, his tongue hanging out, that the assistant threw him out of the shop in disgrace. Knackered when he arrived home, my instructions to him incomplete.'

GOLFING BEE

Yolande Grott was a rookie golfer. She was taking lessons from a Durban course professional, Olufemi Van der Merwe. A month into her daily tuition, Olufemi thought Yolande good off the tee, had good length, a decent stroke, was a competent putter on the greens and a sure feel for scooping her balls from bunkers.

Olufemi thought it was time to encourage Yolande to hit the fairways, that she was ready to tackle 18 holes for the first time. He said to her, 'I am going to pair you with Myrna Smuts, a 20-handicap golfer, for your first round.'

Yolande took to the fairway. Playing better than she imagines she could, she was excited to be a hole up after completing the par-5 first hole. Walking towards the second tee, a bee entered her loose apparel and stung her. The sting was causing Yolande discomfort. She felt as if she could not continue without a painkiller, She Left her golf clubs with Myrna and took a shortcut across a fairway towards the clubhouse and the changing rooms.

Olufemi saw Yolande's hurried approach from his office window. Concerned that she had developed a problem, he was quickly out of the office to ask why she had left the fairways. He asked Yolande, 'What happened. You seem to be in such a panic?'

Yolande said, 'I was stung by a bee between the first and second holes.'

Olufemi replied, sagely, 'Quite obviously, you'll have to learn to keep your feet closer together!'

SNOOKER AN INDIAN INVENTION

Victor the Indian elephant bumped into Siegfried the snake in jungle clearing. Siegfried challenged Victor to participate in a various physical contests, which would entail Victor performing the same feats, but bettering each of Siegfried's challenges.

Siegfried snaked up to a large boulder, tunnelled beneath it, quickly emerging on the other side, ejaculating a long hiss of derision in Victor's direction.

Victor shambled up the boulder and curled his trunk tightly around it. He picked the boulder up, judged its weight with a couple of practice lifts; and then, with ease, tossed it over a tree. The boulder landed with a splash in a river some fifty yards away.

Siegfried approached the spiky with torn roots end of an uprooted tree. He negotiated his slimy body beneath the roots and disappeared. Sixty seconds later, he emerged at the leafless branch end, thirty feet away, hissing, 'Follow that, smartass.'

Victor ambled nonchalantly up to the tree. He rocked the tree with his tusks, then routed his trunk beneath it. With his trunk firmly wrapped around the tree circumference, he picked the entire tree from the ground and tossed it over his shoulder.

Siegfried, realising Victor was earnestly trying to whip his ass, scrambled up Victor's back leg, negotiated a course across his rump, slid around the thick end of his tail and disappeared up his arse. Seconds later, Siegfried reappeared, slipping from Victor's trunk to the ground. Siegfried repeated the feat thrice, each time hissing, 'Follow that Dumbo.'

Victor had had enough. He waited for Siegfried next attempt at negotiating a passage through his intestines. When Siegfried was deep inside his large stomach, Victor contorted his body, stuck his trunk up its arse, and trumpeted, 'Snoooooooooooooker!'

MORE AND MORE SHORTS

Sonia hauled her neighbour's son, 8-yearold Johnny, back to his home. On the doorstep, Sonia said to Johnny's mother, 'I've caught Johnny playing doctors and nurses with my 8-yearold daughter Mary.

Johnny's mother said, 'let's not be too harsh on them, they're only 8 and bound to be curious what the word sex means at that age.'

'Curious about sex, you say,' Sonia said, 'he's just removed Mary's appendix!'

Liam and Mike were having their usual Friday night down the pub. Liam said to Mike, 'I'm off on holiday tomorrow. Would you like me to fetch you back some cigarettes?'

Mike said, 'That's an idea. Fetch me 400 Benson and hedges if you've room in the suitcase.'

Two weeks later, Liam and Mike meet in the pub. Liam said to Mike, 'It was a grand holiday. The weather was good. I was on the beach most days with the children. They loved the freedom of the sands. By the way, Mike, I've your fags. You owe me £149.00.'

Mike said to Liam, 'For fuck sake, where the fuck was you on holiday?'

Liam said, 'Blackpool. Didn't I tell you that?'

Factory owner Jason met his floor sweeper Malky at the local mall. Jason said to Malky, I've been looking around a car showroom for a BMW for my wife. It's her birthday and our wedding anniversary tomorrow. I'm going to look for a diamond eternity ring in the jewellers here for her. If she doesn't like the car, she will still have the ring to wear.

Malky said, 'I'm going to buy my wife a bunch of flowers and a dildo. If she doesn't like the flowers she can go fuck herself!'

Christian hadn't been to the chapel to confess for twenty-years. He didn't know the name of the Father. He took a seat in the booth, looked around, saw the priest enter the other side of the confessional and take a seat. He said to the priest whose outline he could see through the grill. 'Father, things have changed a bit since I last confessed. Now I'm sitting in comfort on a soft-leather armchair. It used to be a rickety, painful on the backside, three-legged stool. There's an optic dispensing whisky by the 50-mil tot, Guinness on tap, pint glasses and some rare porno mags. I could start confessing regularly.'

The priest answered, annoyance spicing his words, 'That's because you're in my side!'

A mother, whilst tidying her 15-yearold son's bedroom room, finds pairs of handcuffs, facemasks, whips, other assorted bondage equipment and fetish mags hidden beneath his bed. The mother asks the boy's dad, 'What do you think I she should do about these items. I don't think it right that our son is interested in using such articles of Sado Masochism.'

Dad replies, I don't know. Whatever you do, do not spank him.

In San Quentin State Prison, it's 8 am on execution day. There's the usual audience seated outside the room of death, watching through the thick glass warders strapping the convicted murderer into the electric chair. The guv'nor approached the high voltage isolator situated on a wall outside the room. He bows his head and throws the switch. The murderer shits himself but survives. The Guv'nor sends for Boris, the electrician. Boris scrambles beneath the chair to check out the circuitry. Easing himself out he throws his arms in the air and shouts, 'This is a fucking death trap!'

Debbie saw a job advertised in the local paper for an intellectual and sensitive woman of culture to work in a body shop. Debbie thought she had the sexiest hands that ever hung on the ends of a woman's wrist. Debbie filled in an application form for the job. Debbie submitted the application form to the body shop. The body shop asked Debbie to attend the body shop for an interview. The body shop offered Debbie the job. Debbie took the job at the body shop.

Debbie has never liked working down at the undertakers.

Dez and his good friend Dave were fishing from a bridge. A cortege of a hearse and two carloads of mourners pass over the bridge. Out of respect for the deceased, Dave stands up, takes off his cap and bows his head. When the cars have passed by, Dave puts his cap back on, sits back down and carries on fishing.

Dez turned to Dave and said, 'Dave, that's one of the nicest most respectful things I've ever seen.'

Dave replied, 'Well I had to show some thought. We were married for nearly 30 years!'

Three house mice, having supped some beer spillage, are bullshitting each other in a Glasgow pub cellar. Haggis, the heighland mouse bragged, 'I'm wise and my reaction time is far too fast for me to be caught in one of the contraptions that human's set to catch us. I go right up to mousetraps, rip away the cheese and snack on it. Then I do thirty bench presses with the trap bar. The spring's never as strong when I'm finished my exercises.

Ken the Lothian mouse said, 'Ken whut yer saying an ah that, but that's fuck aw, ken. I've a grater left ahint by a bawbag junky, ken. Ah grate rat poison and snort it, ken. Does me nae herum, ken.'

Tam the mouse domiciled in a Govan tenement rises to leave. Together, the other mice squeak, 'Where the fuck are ye aff tae Tam?'

'Am awa tae shag the cat,' Tam replied.

On holiday in Thailand, I had a narrow escape. I almost ended up bedding a ladyboy. She looked like a woman, talked like a woman. I didn't suspect a thing, but I got suspicious when she drove back to my hotel safely and parked the car in one slick manoeuvre.

I was in ecstasy with a huge smile on my face. My girlfriend moved forwards, then backwards, forward then backwards, back and forth, back and forth, in and out, in and out. Her heart was pounding, racing, her face flushed. She started to grunt and groan. Suddenly, she let out an almighty scream, 'You park the effing car you smug bastard!'

MORE, MORE AND MORE SHORTIES

Herbert had shafted Dania continuously throughout the day and most of the night, using the doggy fashion position she insisted on each time. Dania was insatiable. He was knackered and, as the bedside alarm chirped for midnight, felt he had earned a good night's sleep. He turned away from Dania and laid his head on a pillow. For the first time he noticed a photo of a man on Dania's bedside cabinet. He instantly began to worry that he might be Dania's husband, who could return at any time and catch him in bed with his wife.

He picked up the photo frame holding the photo, turned to face Dania and asked her, 'Is this your husband?'

'No, silly,' Dania replied and snuggled up to him.

'Your brother?' he enquired.

'No, I have no brothers,' Dania confessed whilst nibbling away at his ear.

'Is it your dad or an uncle?' he inquired. Dania's words were not convincing him.

'No, no, no! You are so hot when you're jealous!' Dania answered.

'Well, who the fuck is he?' he demanded.

Dania whispered in the ear she had just nibbled, 'That's me before my sex change surgery.'

Doctor Foster told me to eat more pasta. On way home from the surgery, I bought some cans of alphabet soup. My girlfriend emptied three cans into a microwaveable dish and heated the contents for our supper.

Quickly after putting away a bellyful of the pasta, I farted. I thought the fart sounded as if someone was trying to converse with me.

My girlfriend must have thought so, too. She asked, 'Was that you asking me to phone you a Neapolitan pizza?'

A woman weightlifter said to her doctor, 'I'm on steroids and have grown a cock.'

Her Doctor asked, 'Anabolic?'

The woman weightlifter answered, 'No, just a cock!'

I went shopping for groceries at our local supermarket this morning. I didn't need much. I bought a pint of milk for my breakfast cereal and coffee and packet of digestives to nibble.

The woman on the till looked an arrogant bitch and so it proved. As I offered my purchases for her to scan she said, 'I can tell you're a single man living in your own.'

'You can tell that from my purchases?' I asked her.

'No,' she replied, 'you're an ugly bastard.'

I rushed home from a hard day at the office. My girlfriend met me at the door of our home. I said to her, 'I was so busy at the office today that I didn't know if I was coming or going.'

My girlfriend replied, 'You must have been going. When you're coming you look like a stroke victim trying to whistle the tiger rag!'

Indian Chief Crazy Horse had a magnificent victory at the Battle of the Little Big Horn, where he defeated General Custer in the battle that historians have dubbed as Custer's Last Stand.

Following his victory, Crazy Horse returned to the Lakota Sioux encampment. During lengthy celebrations of much whooping and much dancing, he drank 75 cups of the hated White Eyes favourite afternoon tipple, tea brewed with Premium P.G. Tips.

The next morning, braves found Crazy Horse dead in his teepee.

The LCCASC, the Limerick Community Council Authentic Sports Committee, has accepted your entry into their All Ireland Turd Curling Championship, held on the city's Bog Flats. To answer any questions competitors may have: you need only to bring your own stool, plenty of opening medicine, a few metres of quality toilet paper and a wheelbarrow to cart away your result at the at the conclusion of your shitting.

Ringaskiddy will hold this year's All Ireland Farting Contest. The battle this year is between reigning champion Rick O'Chet and challenger Wind O'Cord. Past winners of the contest can collect their complimentary pass at the competitor's entrance.

With regard to male entries for our All Ireland How High Can You Piss Contest: the challenge is for wimmen only.

A man watching football match flicked to another channel at half-time to find a porn film, in which a woman was getting a severe, doggy-style rooting. The man said to his wife: I don't know if to continue watching this or return to the football. The wife replied, 'For fuck sake, watch this, you know how to play football!'

Then she sent the cops to question me. The big fat bitch accused me of nicking a pair of her knickers from her line. Apparently, she wasn't too worried about the knickers; she just wanted the 12 pegs returned that stopped them flying off the line like a parachute!

Players from Celtic FC today visited kids on wards at Yorkhill Sick Children's Hospital in Glasgow. It was great to put a smile on the faces of those who face an uphill struggle, said Tommy, aged 5.

A little Liverpudlian lad ran into the house from the backyard. He shouted to his mam, my Liverpool shirt is off the line, lying in the dirt.

His mam went out, looks, and said, 'Some thieving bastard's nicked the pegs!'

I'm sick of double standards: my girlfriend can go out and buy a "Rampant Rabbit dildo" with attachments and she's seen as a naughty fun girl with a new toy. But when I order a 240volt deluxe model fistmaster 5000 latex revolving pussy, with realistic, elasticated anus, imitation shit, a semen overflow tray, wimmen see me as a pervert!

TEDDY BEARS ARE GO

Freddie was a stranger in the town with no local knowledge of where he was likely to meet a girl of his own age out to enjoy herself. He was a blue-eyed kid with blonde hair. Picking up a girl had been easy in the other towns in which he'd gone to work. Asking others boarders using the same digs as he was led him to choose The Jolly Old Fool pub, down near the river, as the pub most likely to provide the entertainment he sought.

Fairground amusements had set up in the car park alongside the river. He wandered the length of the fair. It was a confusion of sounds and flashing lights, parents with screaming kids pushing and shoving desperate to try all the rides. He was pleased to escape into the quietness of a side street, where he found the pub he was looking for.

The pub was jukebox free, was quiet, no raucous rock music blaring out, only one or two old geezers sitting playing dominos. He took them to be local worthies. It wasn't quite what he was looking for in a night out, but the barman conveyed the interesting information that the pub would fill between 9 and 10 as the fair died, shut up shop, the ride and stall operatives packing the pub until closing.

Sure enough, the trickle of customers just after 9pm turned into a deluge of thirsty drinkers crowding into the pub. By 10pm, there were more girls than boys, which pleased Freddie. Sitting on a stool at the end of the bar, he was able to scan the crowd for a pleasant looking girl to chat up. He didn't have to look far. Nelly squeezed in and stood at the bar next to where he was sitting. She was attractive enough with her short hairstyle showing an eager face. She was counting the handful of small change she had taken from a jeans pocket when he tried his luck and said to her, 'Put that away, let me buy you a drink.'

Nelly told Freddie that she ran her parents' stalls at the fair, lived in a large caravan parked behind the pub, where she had all the mod cons needed for a comfortable life travelling to county towns during the fair season.

At closing time, Nelly invited Freddie back to the caravan for a nightcap or coffee, the preference his. In the caravan, it was clear to Freddie that Nelly wasn't about to let him escape her intentions, when she appeared naked at the door of the bedroom, following a trip to the bathroom. He rose from the comfortable seating fitted around the caravan dayroom, took Nelly's hand and allowed her, with little effort, to tug him into the bedroom.

The bedroom was larger than he thought. Freddie saw, in the light thrown out by a bedside lava lamp, that one wall had three shelves fitted onto it. On the top shelf was a row of small teddy bears, all differently dressed. On the middle row, medium sizes teddy bears, all differently dressed. On the bottom shelf, large teddy bears, all differently dressed.

Freddie's immediate thought was that Nelly must be a nice sensitive girl to have collected so many teddies; she might be the one for him.

Freddie cuddled up to Nelly, made love to her all night long in any position of her choosing. He fell asleep exhausted, but awoke as Nelly appeared at his bedside with a steaming mug of milky tea. Freddie sipped at the hot brew and asked Nelly, who had returned to bed, and whose hand was exploring his readiness for another round of passion, 'How was I for you last night?'

'Oh, you weren't too bad,' Nelly replied, 'you can have any prize off the middle shelf!'

MEDIUM TO RARE

Mildred had been a widow for eight weeks and she did so miss her husband Roderick. They had lived a good life together for 55 years, were never apart, except for the war, which he came through unscathed physically, but traumatised.

Mildred's father had fought the Kaiser in the 1914/18 war and had witnessed the angels on the battlefield at Mons. He never mentioned it much fearing derision, but Mildred had seen the light in his eyes as he recounted the tale to her. She believed him implicitly.

Mildred had no qualms about seeking a psychic medium to reach into the afterlife, to Roderick, so she could ask him questions, prove he was there waiting for her arrival, when her time came.

The local Spiritualist Church put Mildred in touch with Rose Lee, a medium of high regard, and very successful in reaching out for those who sought contact with lost souls.

Mildred met Rose Lee at her home in the country, a cottage next to a copse, a gypsy caravan parked nearby, with a sign thereon advertising the high success rate of her mediumship.

Mildred sat across a plain table from Rose Lee as she entered the trance that would take her into the afterlife and to Roderick. After some intonations that Mildred couldn't fathom, Rose Lee jerked, her back stiffening into the upright position, then she spoke, 'I have Roderick here now, Mildred, what would you like me to ask him?'

'Oh, darling Roderick, ask him if he is happy,' Mildred said.

'Yes, he says he is very happy. He also says he keeps his head neat and occasionally has a D.A. He says that you look well,' Rose Lee said.

'Ask Roderick how he fills his day on the other side. He was so active in the garden and at his plot.' Mildred said.

'Roderick says he goes down to the lake each morning and swims until noon. He returns to the banking, eats and makes love all afternoon,' Rose Lee said.

'Ask Roderick why he never did those things with me, please,' asked Mildred, feeling that Roderick had let her down somewhat.

Rose Lee said, 'Roderick says he is now a goosander and will shortly be flying off to warmer climes with his harem!'

SHORTS ON HUMOUR

A gynaecologist lecturing a class of trainee nurses on involuntary muscle spasms asked a student nurse seated in the front row, 'Do you know what your arsehole is doing whilst you're having an orgasm?'

The nurse replied, 'He'd know fuck all about it, he being down at Parkhead watching the Celtic.'

MacDuff lived alone in the wilds of County Angus, with just his dog for company. When the dog died, MacDuff was heartbroken. He visited Reverend Kenzie Mackenzie of the Latter Day Teuchter Church to ask if he could perform a service for the soul of his good and faithful dog.

The reverend replied, 'It is not in our remit to pray or have a service for animals in our church, but the Baptists down the road might not have any beliefs preventing them from saying a prayer for your dog.'

MacDuff said, 'Do you think 5000 pounds would be enough to get them interested?'

Reverend Mackenzie replied, hurriedly, 'For the love of Sweet Mary, Jesus, and all the disciples, why didn't you tell me the dog was a regular attending protestant?'

Peter caught his seven-year-old son Darren trying to nick a biscuit from the barrel. Peter said to him, 'Oi, I wouldn't do that if I were you.'

Darren replied, 'I know that, but I saw you fondling Auntie Sarah's titties whilst mum was at work.'

Peter replied, 'There's some really nice chocolate ones in the fridge.'

An overheard conversation between two nuns, out for a bike ride through the back streets of Rome, went like this: the younger of the two nuns said, 'I've never come this way.'

The older nun said, 'I blame the cobblestones. I always come this way. It's quieter than jogging. I jogged yesterday and heard clapping from behind me. Quickly, I realised it was the cheeks of my arse slapping together, cheering me on.'

Walter was an excessively shy man. He walked into WH Smiths and asked the woman behind the counter, 'Do you have the new self-help book that's out for men with small cocks?'

The woman replied, 'I don't think it's in yet.'

Walter said, 'That's the one. I'll have a copy, please.'

A burial chamber found on a remote Scottish island contained the skeleton of a Viking warrior. In his right hand, he held a mighty, double-edged sword. In the other, he held a betting slip showing a wager of 10 Norwegian Krone on Goliath at even money odds.

Archaeologists state he died from a heart attack.

My live in girlfriend said to me this morning, 'You're the laziest bastard I've ever known. Why don't you pack your bags, fuck off and get some other dozy cow to look after you?'

I said to her, 'You pack them.'

A Glasgow lad took his girlfriend home to meet his parents. He introduced his girlfriend to his father by saying, 'Dad, this is Amanda.'

His father erupts, 'Whit the fuck are ye daein' bringin' a transvestite back here?'

Manchester sewerage workers were on their annual day away to the Lake District. A member of the party fainted in the fresh, rarefied air of the area.

It took 6 buckets of shit to bring him round.

In the early hours, a moaning noise awakened a butcher. Someone was downstairs in the shop. The butcher crept downstairs and quietly entered the shop. He saw his daughter pleasuring herself with a black pudding.

The following day, a customer asked for a black pudding. The butcher said, 'Sorry, I don't have any for sale.'

The Customer said, 'There's a big one hanging on that hook above your head. Can't you see it?'

The butcher replied, 'I can't sell that, it's my new son in law!'

A high street cafe was broken into last night. Thieves stole the kettle and left the interior in a mess.

A police spokesperson said, 'There are tea leaves everywhere.'

I attended a doctor's appointment yesterday and said to him, 'I've a foot that goes to sleep when I'm in bed at night. Nothing I do revitalises it.'

The doctor asked, 'left or right?'

I said, 'The middle one!'

I was sitting with my girlfriend watching a TV program about psychology, with explanations on the phenomenon of mixed emotions.

I turned to my girlfriend and said, 'Honey, that's a bunch of crap. I bet you cannot tell me anything that will make me happy and sad at the same time?'

She said, "Out of all your friends, you have the biggest penis!'

I went around my mate's house last night. He looked glum. 'What's up I asked?'

He replied, 'I've had to put my dog down.'

'Was it ill, hit by a car and injured or was it just old?' I asked.

'Well, er... no...' he stammered. 'I'm too embarrassed to tell anyone why.'

'I'm your mate,' I told him, 'I would never grass on you, no matter what it was.'

'Ok,' he said, in a strained voice, his throat tightening, 'when the wife goes out to the bingo of a night, I plaster Bovril over my bellend and get the dog to lick it off.'

'Dirty bastard,' I responded. 'I can visualise what happened. Your missis came home early and caught you at it.'

'No,' he said, 'My dog looked at me queerly as it tried to get its cock into the Bovril jar.'

FOLLOWING ON

I once had a Chinese girlfriend. She would take me to bed, but I couldn't get her interested in blowjobs or sixty-nines. Then I had a great idea that worked: I learned some Cantonese lingo. When I said hey you, two can choo, I choo and you choo too, life was wonderful.

I had a house surveyor around. He said, 'Take the old boiler out.'
    I said, 'She doesn't like going down the pub.'

Wallet fraud warning: two, fit, eighteen-year old girls, of eastern origin, wearing tight, tiny tops and bottoms, may approach males in supermarket car parks. They wash your car windscreen with their tits hard pressed against it. Then they will ask for a lift to the next nearest supermarket. En route, they will strip off and perform oral sex on each other. One will climb to the front of the car and perform oral sex on you, whilst the other steals your wallet. I had my wallet stolen last Monday, Tuesday, Wednesday and Twice on Thursday. I'm shopping there again tomorrow. So be careful.
    PS wallets are 99p each in Quidstretchers!

A lifeguard at the local swimming pool said to me today, 'You dirty little fucker you'll have to leave. The large bulge in your Speedos is upsetting the other swimmers.'
    I pointed out another male, in similar trunks, with a similar bulge, and asked, 'Why is he not being removed unceremoniously from the pool?'

The lifeguard said, 'He hasn't shit himself like you have!'

I went down the pub last night; the missis went to bed early. The dog was snoring badly and she couldn't sleep. She had heard from a dog-loving friend that tying a ribbon around a dog's bollocks was a sure way to stop the disturbing, canine racket. It worked and she eventually fell asleep.

I lumbered in after midnight, having had quite a skinfull, and tumbled into bed. I'm a terrifying snorer and although it never wakes me up, the clamour wakes the missis. I didn't want a bollocking for that or for being late home. I did my best and stayed awake until I couldn't keep my eyes open any longer and fell asleep quickly.

One loud, drunken snore woke the missis and, knowing that a ribbon wrapped round the dog's bollocks worked, the missis searched for another ribbon and tied a blue one round mine.

In the morning, I spotted the ribbons. I said to the dog, 'I don't know where we pair was last night, but it seems we've come first and second in a competition!

10-o'clock news: Scottish islanders give the name Celtic to a beached whale. Apparently, there's similarities in the two stories: both club and beast had floundered, were in a no win situation, were dead out of the water, were marooned without hope, had hit hard the buffers of desire, had the wind taken from both their blowpipes, were both in their death throes.

The Very Reverend Cannon Ranger of the Ibrox Diocese will pray for them at the requiem.

BELIEFS OF TODAY

Terry wished to place an advert in the Dating Magazine for the Pious, which his local church endorsed. Miss Edna Trubody, Church Elder and head of the church Self-Help Group, sought clarification regarding the shorthand insertions he wished to include in his advert.

Edna wrote, Dear Terry, we hope that you, too, have a G.S.O.H. However, the following are not amongst previous date seeker's requirements that we recognise. To assess correctly what type of partner you are seeking, we need to know the inferences contained in the following: U.T.A. B.J. M.D. W. F. and G.R?

Edna.

HIGH DIRTY WATER MARK
REACHED

Doctor Antonio had received in an email from the clinic containing the worrying result of Reverend Father Alfresco Beaujolais' testicular and urinary tract scan. Doctor Antonio had his receptionist arrange an appointment for Father Alfresco, at times that he would not be concerned with any daily Mass; he also needed the privacy and security of the surgery to reveal the scan results. He did not know how Alfresco would react to the radiographer's findings.

In the surgery and comfortably seated, Father Alfresco listened intently to Doctor Antonio's words. 'Your scan has shown up a nasty, testicular and urinary tract condition. I'm afraid to tell you, for fear of eternal, fiery damnation, there is only one recognised cure of which I know.'

'My son,' Father Alfresco said, looking benignly towards the doctor, 'have no fears. I'm sure my back is strong enough to handle your diagnosis and my system to cope with the necessary medicine, whatever they may be.'

'Father Alfresco, the only cure known to medical science is for you to have sexual intercourse: a wild rooting session, many and prolonged ejaculations, with a strapping woman. A rooting session so severe that not even a Borgia, for which that blighted family were famous, would contemplate performing in a moment of sexual madness. I recommend sexual congress with a woman, a hussy skilled in extracting ejaculatory fluids. A woman to bring blessed relief, to release years of pent up frustrations of the soul and to reduce the high, dirty-water mark flooding your body. The accumulation of semen straining to burst your bulging testes and epididymis has made these unused body parts look like the boiled eyes of a blue whale. For a complete cure, you will undoubtedly need a strong back, my silence and god's forgiveness, too.'

'Doctor Antonio, friend, confidant, if that is the only way I can live out my natural days, continue doing my Holy work, serve my congregation, then I must take the plunge and chance God's wrath. However, there will be four conditions. The woman must be blind, so she cannot see me, deaf so she cannot hear me and mute so she cannot ask me any questions.'

'And what is your fourth condition, Father Alfresco,' the doctor asked the hesitating Father.

'She must have massive tits, a cuddly arse and a lovely shaven fanny.'

SILLY ONELINERS

Looking out of my window, I spot people gathering around a man fallen from his motorbike. Frantic, I rushed over, shouting, 'Out of my way,' I barged a route between gawping bystanders and made my way to the accident site.

A woman asked me, 'Are you a doctor?'

I said, 'No. He was delivering my pizza!'

During my shift at the chemists, a customer picked up some naked photos of a woman. Naturally, I'd had a peak at them. 'Would you like the negatives?' I asked.

The customer looked at me sheepishly and answered, 'Yes please.'

I said, 'Ok, then, your friend has saggy tits, a fat arse and her fanny needs trimming.'

The venue boss sacked me from my job as a bingo caller last night. Apparently, a meal for two with a hairy view isn't an acceptable description for the number 69!

When I arrived at my girlfriend's pad last night, she had two of her mates visiting. 'Here he is,' she said, excitedly, 'we were just talking about having a foursome, if you're up for it. We were waiting for you to arrive.'

Two minutes later, I appeared, naked, hard on in my hand, at the ready. They had tennis rackets in theirs!

A religious education class in a Glasgow school: Young Mary asked the teacher, 'Do angels fly, miss?'

'Dae they fuck,' Young Jimmy shouted, in what he thought was a know-all voice.

'One question at a time,' said the teacher.

Father Donovan confessed that when the prospective bride asked him what the Church's attitude to oral sex was, he said did not know what oral sex was. The prospective bride showed him.

Now, when prospective brides ask the same question, he never says he knows what oral sex is!

My missis left me a note on the TV set. It said, 'It's not working. I'm off.'

I plugged it in, turned it on. There was nothing wrong with it…..silly woman.

Sean bought a chainsaw that guaranteed he could cut down and trim 40 trees per hour. At best, he could only manage 20. He took the chainsaw back to the tool store to complain. He said to the tool-storekeeper, 'I've only ever been able to cut down and trim 20 trees an hour with this machine which you guaranteed would do 40.

The tool-storekeeper twiddled with the carburettor, pulled the start cord and the saw clattered into life.

Sean said, 'What's that fucking noise it's making now?'

I took Bruno my Rottweiler to the vet's surgery 'My dog's cross-eyed. Is there anything you can do for him?' I asked the Vet

'Let's have a look at him,' the Vet said and picked the dog up. The Vet examined his eyes, and checked his teeth. 'I'm going to have to put him down now,' he said.

'Why? Because he's cross-eyed? 'I asked the vet.

'No, because he's really heavy,' the Vet said.

I went to a doctor's appointment. The doctor said, 'Don't eat anything fatty for a week.'

I asked, 'Do you mean stuff like sausage and bacon?'

The doctor said, 'No, Fatty, don't eat anything for a week.'

I knocked at my friend's door. His wife Dorothy answered. I said 'Is Jim at home?'

Dorothy didn't reply, just stood there looking at me.

I was about to ask again when another woman appeared at Dorothy's side. 'Sorry luv,' she said, 'we buried him last Thursday.'

'Did he mention the pot of paint he borrowed before he went?' I asked.

I went to Blackpool on holiday. I knocked on the door of the first hotel I came to. A woman stuck her head out of an upstairs window and shouted down to me, 'What do you want?'

'I'd like to stay here,' I said.

'Ok. Stay there,' she said.

I went to the doctor. He said, 'You have got a very serious illness.'

I said, 'I want a second opinion.'
He said, 'All right, you're ugly as well.'

I went into this pub, and I ate a ploughman's lunch. He was livid.

I got home from work and the wife said, 'I'm very sorry dear, but the cat's eaten your dinner,'
I said, 'Don't worry I'll get you a new cat.'

I bumped into an old school friend in the pub last night. He was looking a bit glum. I asked him what was up.

'I can't afford anything anymore,' he sighed. 'I've had to cancel my golf and gym memberships, my William Hill and Ladbroke's accounts, reduce my Sky TV package and ditch my tri-monthly wine order from Laithwaites. Fags I've cut to 20 a week. My wife cut up our credit cards.'

'Because of the recession we're having?' I asked.

'No, he replied, 'I've been forced off benefits and had to get a job.'

Tommy got suspended from school today. The teacher asked him if he had £20 and he gave Joanne, Claire and Katie £5 each what would you have at the end. Apparently, 3 blowjobs and enough left for a kebab was the wrong answer.

NOAH'S TESTIMONY

Noah, a seasoned Texan farmer, was travelling along a narrow road, a loaded stock trailer attached to his pickup. An 18-wheeler Mack rig, overtaking a bicycle and on the wrong side of the road, collided with the pickup and stock trailer, with tragic consequences.

Noah's case, to seek compensation for the destruction of his vehicles and the destroying of his heifer, went to court. The truck company's hotshot lawyer, attempting to muddle Noah's testimony, began his questioning. 'At the scene of the accident, is it true that you spoke to the police officer in attendance and you said to him, and I quote your exact words, 'I am fine,'

Noah replied, 'Your honour, I'll explain what occurred. I loaded a young heifer and was taking her to a neighbouring farm where a sturdy bull, of the same breed, with renowned testicles, would mate with her.....'

I didn't ask for any details', the
lawyer interrupted. 'Just answer the question. Did you not say to the police officer, attending the accident scene, 'I am fine?'

Noah said, 'Your honour, as I was trying to explain, I loaded the heifer into the trailer and I was driving along the road.... '

The lawyer interrupted again, turned to the judge and said, 'Your Honour, I am trying to establish the fact that, at the scene of the accident, the plaintive told the police officer, he was fine. He is now trying to sue my client for damages to his pickup, his trailer, his heifer and to his person. I believe he is a fraud.'

The Judge was from farming stock and interested in Noah's answer. He said to the lawyer, 'I'd like to hear what he has to say about the accident. Proceed.'

Noah nodded to the Judge and said, 'As I was saying, your honour, before shylock here rudely interrupted me. I had just loaded the heifer into the trailer and on my way to the other farm. The truck was on the wrong side of the road as it came around the corner ahead of me. I didn't have time to take avoiding action. It hit the pickup and the trailer. The force of the collision threw me through the pickup windscreen. I landed in a ditch alongside the heifer. I was hurt bad. I ached all over and didn't want to move. I had to lie in bed for a week to recover. The heifer was bleeding from her neck. The way her spine was twisted, it was broken. She just lay there, making terrible noises, in agony, in terrible pain, your honour.

'Then a policeman on a motorbike turned up. He could obviously see there was no hope for the heifer. He took his gun from its holster and put a bullet between her eyes, to put her out of her misery.

'The policeman turned to me, the gun still in his hand, and asked, 'How are you feeling?' Your honour, what would you have said?'

DICK'S SECTION

Wee Marjorie was out for a ride near her home, on the edge of town, on her stabilised tricycle.

Mounted Police Officer, Richard Dick, out exercising his horse, stopped and spoke to Marjorie. 'Is that your bike you are riding,' Officer Dick asked.

'Yes,' Marjorie replied.

'You will have to get a reflector fitted to your back mudguard,' Officer Dick instructed, 'if I catch you out again on it I will have to fine you for the offence.'

Marjorie asked Officer Dick, Is that your horse?'

'Yes,' said Officer Dick.

'Well,' Marjorie said, 'I'd take it back, if I were you. A horse is supposed to have a prick hanging between its back legs, not sitting in the saddle!'

Sex-education-class teacher Ivor Dick drew a penis on the blackboard. He said to the class, 'Can anyone tell me what this is?'

Henry stuck up his hand and piped up, 'My Dad has two of them.'

'Surely not,' the surprised teacher said.

'Yes he has,' confirmed Henry, 'he has a small one for peeing with and a big one for cleaning the babysitter's teeth!'

Leading pharmaceutical company Dickophilo has invented a drug to treat the depression inherent in dick-shy lesbians.

The company will market the drug under the label TriDixagin.

Sunday tabloid, The Daily Dick, encouraging men to consider sperm donation, concluded: most men have a dirty handkerchief stashed beneath their bed, which would fulfil that need, had they not let the precious fluid trickle through their fingers.

Dick decided to become a professional boxer. His manager sends him for a medical. Ten days later, th manager told him he has sugar diabetes. Dick said, 'No problem, I'll knock him out in the first round.'

Dick was drinking with his mate Dolph in the bar of the hotel at which they were staying. He had the sudden urge to urinate and left Dolph to find the Gents. In the Gents, the sight of a condom machine had Dick thinking. There were some good-looking girls drinking in the bar. He was sure one or two of them had given him the eye, but he was unsure that there might be only one of them and she was cockeyed. Dick had never had sex and had no need to buy condoms, but he though, to be ready for any eventuality, he should buy a pack.

Dick was gone for some time and Dolph thought he'd better check upon his friend. In the gents, he found Dick stuck up against the condom machine. 'What the devil are you trying to do, Dick,' Dolph asked, concerned at his mate's plight.

'The machine said put 2 quid in the slot and push in the knob,' Dick said, 'That's what I did, but something inside the machine won't let go!'

Dick was a stranger in the town. In the pub in which Dick chose to have a drink, the woman sitting alone on a stool at the bar was the only friendly face he saw.

She wasn't the worst looker he'd ever chatted up and she seemed eager to have a conversation with him. He bought her a few drinks and they were getting on well. At throwing out time, she invited him to stay the night with her at her nearby apartment. Dick of course agreed and walked hand in hand to her place.

They ended up in bed as he'd expected. During foreplay, she said to him between blowing her hot breath into an ear, 'You've the biggest cock I've ever laid my hands on.'

Dick said to her, 'You're pulling my leg!'

Dick's girlfriend said to him, 'You're much too childish for me to ever have a decent mature conversation with you. We're going to have a serious talk about it.'

Dick was hoping she doesn't pick a time during the conker season!

In another town where Dick was a stranger, in a pub where he spotted a girl sitting alone on a stool at the bar, he sidled up to her nonchalantly and said to her, 'Do you suck cock.'

She replied, 'Dick, It's never entered my head.'

Town number two where Dick was a stranger, sitting on a stool at the bar of a pub, a woman approached him and asked, 'Dick, do you have a big cock?'

Dick replied, 'The ten-and-one-half-inch thing I keep in my underpants is a skidmark!'

Town number three, where Dick was a stranger, a woman picked him up in a pub and took him home to her flat. The woman left him sitting on her sitting room to go and change out of her clothing. She reappeared naked brandishing a whip. Let's get into some kinkiness, she said to Dick, cracking the whip to emphasise what she expected from him.

Dick replied, 'I've wanked off your dog, shit in your fish tank and pissed in your handbag. How kinkier do you want me to be?'

In the fourth town where Dick was a stranger, he visited the home of work colleague Dave, recuperating there from a broken leg.

Dave requested Dick to go upstairs for him and fetch his slippers for him, as his feet were cold. Upstairs, Dick finds Dave's twin teenage daughters sitting together on a bed. 'Hello girls,' Dick greets them, 'your dad sent me up to shag you both, which one of you wants me first?'

'Fuck off,' both daughters cry out in unison.

'I'll prove it,' Dick replied, and shouted downstairs to Dave, 'both of them?'

'Of course,' Dave shouted back, 'what use is one.'

In the fifth town where Dick was a stranger, he had tried to be careful entering the hotel lift; nature had decreed that he would forever be an awkward oaf. He apologised sincerely to the woman stood next to him, as his elbow caught her breast as he turned to face the door.

The woman smiled at him and said, 'If your cock is as hard as your elbow, I'm in room 36.'

8 KINDS OF SEX

The 1st kind of sex is Smurf Sex. This kind of sex happens when you first meet someone, and you both have sex until you are blue in the face.

The 2nd kind of sex is Kitchen Sex. This is when you have been with your partner for a short time, and you are so needy you will have sex anywhere, even in the kitchen.

The 3rd kind of sex is Bedroom Sex. This is when you have been with your partner for a long time. Your sex has become routine and you usually have sex only in your bedroom

The 4th kind of sex is Hallway Sex This is when you have been with your partner for too long. When you pass each other in the hallway, you both say 'Fuck you.'

The 5th kind of sex is Religious Sex. Which means you get Nun in the morning, Nun in the afternoon and Nun at night?

The 6th kind is Courtroom Sex. This is when you cannot stand your wife any more. She takes you to court and screws you in front of everyone.

The 7th kind of sex is Social Security Sex. You get a little each month, but not enough to enjoy yourself.

The 8th kind of sex is In Prison Sex. If your cellmate requests you play mummies and daddies with him and you say you don't fancy being mummy, your cell mate will say, 'Will daddy come and suck mummy's cock!'

SEX IN THE DARK AND OTHER PLACES

A couple had been married for 20 years. Every time they had sex together, the husband insisted on performing in darkness and turned off the lights.

After 20 years, the wife thought lights out routine ridiculous. She promised herself that she would break her husband's crazy habit. During their next sex session, although it was enjoyable, she was able to find the switch and turned on the lights. Looking down her naked body, she saw that her husband was using a battery-operated vibrator to make love to her. It felt hard, wonderful, larger than, but not the real thing.

She pushed her husband and the thing away from her and shouted, 'You're impotent. How could you have lied to me all of these years? I think you should explain yourself.'

The husband looked her straight in the eye and said calmly, 'I'll explain the toy. You explain our kids.'

When the missis left, I was sad, upset and lonely. Since then I've got a dog, a Harley, had sex with three wimmen and blown a grand on drink and cocaine.

She'll do her nut when she comes home from work.

I thought my new girl friend might be the one for me. However, looking through her knicker drawer, and finding a nurse's outfit, a policewoman's uniform and a French maid's outfit. I've changed my mind. If she cannot hold a job down, she's not the one for me.

I think the saying, 'As tight as a duck's arse' raises a serious issue: Who was responsible for finding that out!

Ornithologists say owls have the keenest hearing on the planet. Surely, they've never tested a husband watching porn whilst his wife sleeps.

A man phones an Airfix model shop and asks the shopkeeper, 'Do you have any models of Italian cruise liners?'

'Yes,' said the shopkeeper, 'I've only one left.'

'Will you put it on one side for me?' asked the man.

A wife was sitting on the patio with her husband, sipping wine from a glass. Lifting her head, she said, 'I love you so much. I don't know how I could ever live without you.'

The husband said, 'Is that you or the wine talking?'

The wife replied, 'I was talking to the wine.'

Muff diving aficionados, from all nations, will swoop into Ringaskiddy this weekend to contest the All Ireland, prestigious, Fury Cup contest. Unfortunately, some exhibitionist contestants disqualified themselves last year. This year, organisers have barred the 'mad dog eating tripe' technique from this year's competition.

Women are also in the mix in this popular sporting weekend. However, organisers have barred

Mary Murphy from entering the 'Ladies Splits' contest.

Apparently, having a fanny shaped like a ripped out fireplace, they thought was too great an advantage over other less stretch-worthy contestants.

NICKNAMES AND THEIR ORIGINS

Two Soups: real name Campbell Baxter.

Two Bonnets: is someone wearing a wig beneath their hat.

Colostomy: is the girl a married man is poking; namely, the wee bag on the side.

Boomerang: whenever anyone at their work asks a question, they always reply, 'I'll get back to you on that.'

Parachute: they let everyone down at the last minute.

Cashline: is an experienced woman open for business 24 hours a day.

Vaseline: his real name is Willie Burns.

Bo Derek: Derek has a terrible body odour.

Brewer's Droop: his real name is Willie Down.

Genie: they magically appear whenever anyone opens a bottle.

Dulux: their friends reckon they have only one coat.

Soapy: they wash their hands of any problems that crop up.

Yeti: they are always off work on the sick. There have been many unconfirmed sightings of them, but nobody can prove they actually exist.

Gas Man: it's believed he services old boilers.

Hostage: if anyone asks them for help, they always reply, 'Sorry, my hands are tied.'

Chernobyl: during the mid-eighties, Bill had a bad complexion.

Woodpecker: they are always tapping.

Mussolini: is an immoral woman: the Great Dicktaker.

Olympic Flame; is the girl you like, but will never go out with you.

GIRLFRIENDS

Last night, I walked Eva home to her apartment. In her living room, a cat was sitting on a settee purring. I said to Eva, 'You'll be doing that when I get you into bed.' Unfortunately, when she turned round, the cat was licking its arse!

Belinda, my latest girlfriend, asked me, 'What *is* that white powder plastered over your bell end?' as she viewed my erect penis from her pillow.

'It's aspirin, I explained, 'It's for your headache. 'How would you like to receive the dosage?' I asked, 'orally or anally?'

Marjorie, the new girlfriend I share an apartment with, sent me a text that said she was in Casualty. When I got home, I watched all 30 minutes of the soap whilst enjoying a few beers. I never saw Marjorie once. That girl's a liar.

She still hasn't come home and I'm starving.

I was singing to a prospective girlfriend that I met last Saturday night. She said, 'You sound like Johnny Cash.'

I asked, 'You mean like the man in black?'

She said, 'No. Like changes spewing from a condom machine!'

Dinah entered my local boozer last night on crutches. Apparently, she plays rugby and suffered head injuries when the maul fell on top of her on Saturday afternoon. Then she broke her Calcaneus, a major foot bone and lost her purse, when she fell down the stairs at the rugby club pissed.

She's not well heeled nowadays and cannot give head. She's not for me.

Miranda disappeared from my love life quite quickly. She said she'd like something made out of animal skin for her birthday;

She was none too pleased with the donkey jacket.

I really fancied Sally, my sexy next-door neighbour, until she called to confront me about washing going missing from her line.

I nearly shit her pants.

I'd gone through a few girlfriends by the time I met Mirabelle. Then she complained that I never brought her flowers. In Aldi, I bought her self-raising and plain. You should have seen the look she gave me when she told me I was a miserable sod!

I was learning fast, so I bought Margarita a pug dog. Despite the squashed nose, wonky eyes and all the slavering, the dog seems to like her.

Recently, I've notice my voice has deepened. I'm sure it's to do with my new choice of undergarments. I've gone from Y-fronts to the scrotal looseness boxer shorts offers.

However, if there has been significant lowering in my testicular department, I hope it doesn't mean I'm going to grow up.

SHORTIES FROM THE MIDDLE SHELF

Marmaduke Story;
Teacher: 'Four crows are perched on the fence. The farmer shoots one. How many are left?'
Marmaduke: 'None.'
Teacher: 'That's not correct.'
Marmaduke: 'There's None.'
Teacher: 'Explain that answer?'
Marmaduke: 'The farmer shoots one crow; the others hear the bang and fly off.'
Teacher: 'That isn't the correct answer, but I like the way you think.'
Marmaduke: 'Teacher, can I ask you a question?'
Teacher: 'Sure. Go ahead.'
Marmaduke: 'There are three women in the ice cream parlour. One is licking at an ice cream cone, one is biting it and one is sucking on it. Which one is the married woman?'
Teacher: 'The one sucking the cone.'
Marmaduke: 'No. The one with the wedding ring on, but I like the way you think.'

Sex therapists' recommendation: the quickest way to arouse a man is for a woman to lick his earlobes.
    Personally, I think it's bollocks.

Taking a line from the world of boxing, members of the canine showing judging fraternity have stated that a championship contender must show a presence in the ring.
    However, I've never seen a cross-eyed boxer win a prize at a dog show.

I had requested a male doctor for this diagnosis. During his investigation, he found the lump on my bollocks that had bothered me.

He concluded that there was nothing to worry about, saying, 'The lump on your right testicle is a blob of chewing gum. It's what you get when the girl giving you a blow job is trying to quit smoking!'

During a nursing degree course lecture at a Glasgow college on muscular spasms, the lecturer, rather offhandedly, asked a female student, 'Do you know what your arsehole is doing when you're having an orgasm?'

The nurse replied 'He's probably at Parkhead watching Celtic!'

A young man went to the surgery complaining about his sore arse. After a full rectal examination, the doctor explained: a normal body has 206 bones; temporarily, it seems yours has had 207.

Grandad went into a nursing home. I rang and asked, 'How is he doing?'

A nurse said, 'He's like a fish out of water.'
I asked, 'Is he finding it hard to adjust?'
Nurse said, 'No, he's dead!'

SHORTIES FROM THE TOP SHELF

My mother told me once that, before I was born, she thought I was masturbating in her womb. I retorted, 'Why in heaven's name did you think that?'

Mother replied, 'Well, you never made a footballer did you, Fatso!'

Apparently, I was born with an erection. The midwife had to smack me around the bell end with a twelve-inch ruler before she could get my first nappy on!

My first school was in the adjacent village to the one in which I grew up. After the war, my mother took an afternoon job as a maid, at a farm situated between the two villages. At the end of the school day, I would call at the farm to await my mother finishing work and walk home with her.

A flock of turkeys roamed the farmyard. I was no taller than the largest of the birds. I saw them as a threat to my safety; I was scared of them and the racket they made.

Once, while I waited for mum to finish work, my dad arrived at the farm on his bike. I said to dad, 'I don't like the noise these turkeys are making.'

Dad spoke words to me that, even today, I do not understand. His words weren't reassuring at all. He said, 'Never mind son. When you grow up, you will love the sound of a gobble!'

I was always in trouble as a wee boy. At Sunday school, I dropped a stink bomb. The congregation exited quickly. The priest thought it was a weapon of mass destruction.

Order arms means something completely different to a cannibal commando

Take a stool means something very different to a dung spreader.

The last time I saw a pair of legs like yours, a Frenchman was ripping them from a frog.

The last time I saw a pair of legs like yours they were hanging out of a vulture's nest.

I tried chatting up this loose woman in a bar last night. I couldn't get a meaningful conversation going with her: every 2 minutes she pissed off for a crap.

My girlfriend wants to get on TV's Deal or no Deal. She says it's the last chance she'll have of finding anything big in her box.

My latest girlfriend is the noisiest woman I know. She's on the short list to go around the deepest dug graveyards when they start wakening up the dead.

I paid £250 for an amber broach for a girlfriend. I asked the girl behind the jeweller's counter why it was so expensive. She politely told me, 'Sir, it has a fly encapsulated in it.'
  I asked, 'Is there enough room in it for a zip?'
  Pissed her off a bit, it did.

I was down the pub with a few of my drinking friends last night. When I arrived home, I was more pissed than a nursing home chair.

Female opera singers should only be allowed to make that caterwauling sound when they're having an orgasm.

The latest period drama a TV company will show relates to a bad week in Shrewsbury.

On a cruise, I was walking around the promenade deck when I bumped into the captain. He didn't mind so I bumped into him again.

BUSINESS TRIP TO JAPAN

I was on a business trip to Japan, staying in a Tokyo city centre hotel. Out for a walk that Saturday afternoon, I noted there was plenty to see on the vibrant streets. The flashing lights, sumo-wrestling venues, sushi parlours where I could sample gourmet fish dishes, were not an attraction to me.

That night, feeling lonely alone in my hotel room, I decided to seek companionship from one of the very attractive girls I had noted offering sexual services in the city's red light district.

Sakura tempted me into a flirtation. She was young and lovely. Dressed in a light kimono and jacket, with almond shaped eyes and black hair, standing about 5-foot 4-inches tall with nice titties, she stood out from the other girls offering their bodies. We walked hand in hand to the hotel, walked innocently past reception into the lift and up to my tenth floor hotel suite.

We had no common language, but Sakura, being the complete professional, knew her business and peeled off her clothing whilst I used the toilet and stripped. On my return, she was naked, on her knees, on the bed, posing in the classic doggy style position. I did not think she was praying and did not prolong her wait. I was ready and approached her enticing rear end slowly, with reverence. It was nice and firm. I kissed it on both cheeks. Then I mounted her and began thrusting.

Quite quickly, Sakura joined me in a rhythmic union, wiggling her backside back and forth and doing press ups, whilst I held her close to me. I thought to myself, Sakura is really enjoying my lovemaking.

Then, quite suddenly, Sakura began hollering words in Japanese that I had not heard before: 'Machigatta ana, machigatta ana, machigatta ana,' she repeated.

My immediate thought was that she was congratulating me in her language for the great rooting I was doing.

I speeded up my thrusting and finished quite quickly after Sakura's outburst. I paid for her short time services, adding a few extra Yen because of her appreciation of me. Then I took her down to street level and waved goodbye to her as she toddled off towards the red light district, no doubt looking for another customer.

That night, I slept untroubled until the light of morning awoke me.

I needed a translator for the business deals I was pursuing in Tokyo. My firm had arranged my collection on Sunday morning by translator Haruki. He would drive me to a golf course for a round and take me for lunch in the clubhouse.

I had a decent handicap at my local course, but I was no march for Haruki. He had a longer drive and his putting was near perfect. On the 11th hole, a par 5, Haruki teed off, sending his ball right up to the flag. I was amazed at the strength in his drive and accuracy. I thought I should congratulate him. I also thought it a nice touch if I used the only words in Japanese that would convey sincerity in my praise.

I said to Haruki, 'Machigatta Ana.'

Haruki approached me looking puzzled. 'Rob,' he said, 'why you say to me wrong hole?'

AVIAN SPHINCTRE ART

Picture the scene:

A Lancaster Bomber is on a raid over Cologne, Germany, 22:00 hours, December 1944. The Bomb Aimer is in position. He has taken the advice from the Navigator that the craft is nearing the target. The Pilot relays the speed of approach. Flak explosions begin to illuminate the darkened fuselage.

The Bomb Aimer has already calculated wind speed and drift. His calculations tell him exactly when he must release the devastation the Lancaster carries, so that the target he now sees through his bombsight is properly blitzed. The Bomb doors open. To the best of his abilities and knowledge, he presses the button to release the bombs. The Lancaster leaps as the weight drops away, the bombs looping in a fine arc before plummeting towards their intended target.

Alternative scenario:

A seagull takes off from the landfill its belly heavy with potential bombs. It assumes a well-known flight path and wings towards the river running through the town. It douses itself in the river's fast-flowing, pristine waters, sheds landfill stench and filth from its feathers. Then it flies to a favourite roost to continue preening.

En route to the favoured building, the avian brain calculates when to release the bomb, without the assistance of instruments or advice from others. Inherent, birdbrain knowledge tells the bird when it should, with accuracy, "nip one off", as it glides on a steady, slowing, ascending curve towards its intended roost above my patio doors. The bomb lands exactly

239

on my window, revealing, unexpectedly, artistic, avian skills.

How can that be? From where does this art materialise? Where does the bomb transform into a daub, assume artistic potential? Does the avian brain create the art? Does the avian brain issue an instruction to the sphincter, to contort precisely, to shape the nipped-off bomb? The daub, on contact with the canvas, depicts accurately the avian thought, as art. Surreal!

Does the daub, during its short passage through the atmosphere to the intended canvas, receive ethereal instruction from an avian divine source?

The answer is, in the end, for you to decide.

Examples of avian art included.

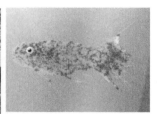

ALL COPPERS ARE BASTARDS

You would be excused your incredulity that piles were anything to do with police duty, or of the tale I am about to relate; I shall explain the first reason that they do.

On a male recruit's final interview and medical to become a police officer, he has to strip to his boxers, parade in front of a bench of top cops, drop the shorts, turn, bend over, grip his nether cheeks, pull them apart and leave his ringpiece on view until the bench give haemorrhoidal judgement. Evidence of the grapelike, blood-gorged sphincter protuberances is a non-starter to a career of plodding the beat.

I will now commence this true tale. Picture a narrow, covered arcade, perhaps of twenty-five paces long, that gave pedestrian passageway between two streets. In the arcade, two businesses traded. To one side of the arcade length a jeweller's doorway and a cafeteria, both in recesses. Both doorways were unlit during the hours of darkness. Secured to the opposite wall of the arcade length, the gable end of a busy pub, two rectangular display cabinets stood.

In the early hours of a dry, summertime, Friday nightshift, two young, duty-minded coppers, chose to use the arcade as a shortcut to their patrolling of the other street, both streets being parts of their beat. In the darkness, the coppers noticed their boots were slopping through puddles that had formed on the passageway cement. At the cafeteria doorway, torchlight exposed the reason. It took little speculation. At closing time, male beer drinkers were testing their bladder strength and its capacity; namely, pissing its contents as far as they could into the cafeteria. Lining up the eye of their bellends to the quarter-inch gap between the glass doors, they jetted urine into the cafeteria interior, soaking tables and chairs. The puddles on the cement were urine that had seeped back through the gap beneath the doors.

Second reason: old coppers walk slower than their younger colleagues do. It is a little known formula, outwith police forces, that the speed of an old copper's walk is directly proportional to the excitation of his piles. Pounding beats for years is a well-known cause of the sphincter irritation and few old plods reach retirement without requiring prescriptions of an anal-itch easing treatment.

Had two haemorrhoid-bearing coppers used the arcade that night, their slower walk would have caused fewer urine splashes. Their dull boots were unlikely to tarnish as their younger colleagues did, and there would be no story for me to tell.

The two younger coppers, more than slightly miffed that their heavily bulled boots had received an unwarranted pish wash, decided that, after last orders in the pub on Saturday night, whilst they were on nightshift, someone would suffer a penalty for the irritation and the attention they'd to give to re-bulling their boots.

Saturday nightshift, as the pub barman called closing time, the two young coppers were out of sight, in the darkened jeweller's doorway, waiting to pounce on a victim. They didn't have to wait long. A lad of about twenty years, dressed for a summer's day, came dashing around the corner into the darkened arcade. He did not choose to top up the cafeteria urine reservoir. Instead, he walked into the gap between the

242

two display cabinets. On the sound of urine hitting the floor, the two young coppers leapt out from their hideaway, torches blazing, lighting up the dampish area of the offence. The lad, in deep shock and in some pain, his foreskin bulbous, had squeezed the loose skin, between finger and thumb, and had ceased urination.

The lead copper on this investigation, in the friendliest manner he could muster, as the situation confronting him had turned humorous, stifled a chortle. He had heard a choked snigger from his number two. They both were guilty of using any old sheltered spot for a slash whilst out on beat duty during the hours of darkness.

Eventually the lead copper said, 'Had I the mind to do so, I could arrest you for this. As he was speaking, a courting couple, arm in arm, walked past, without paying heed to the situation. The lead copper, continuing his assessment of the situation, said, 'Because those two people passed by, I could now arrest you on the more serious charge of breach of the peace. However, I'm not going to do so. I just want you never to do anything like this again.'

The lad said, in a grateful voice, 'Thank you officer, I won't. Can I now finish my slash here?'

The copper said, loudly, 'No you cannot.'

The lad asked, 'Where can I finish? The pub is now closed.'

'Go out of here onto the High Street. Turn left, two hundred yards up, cross the duel carriageway, two streets further on, on the right, you will find an open Gents, next to the town hall.'

With those directions reverberating in his ears, the lad put his unoccupied hand down the inside of his

243

trousers, negotiated with extreme care his bulging foreskin through the fly with the other, pulled up the zip, and walked, a free man, but uncomfortably, towards the public toilet.

Not all coppers are bastards!

I hope you agree.

OMEGA

VIRAL THOUGHTS

56 days ago, I had a Covid-19 vaccine jab in my upper left arm. No ill effects there; but, within hours of the needle, my right arm became detached from my torso. It just dropped off, didn't say it was going.

On reaching the floor of my apartment, my arm began circulating using four fingers as digital motability. My arm evaded capture, hopping over my Juliette balcony surround with ease. It left behind a bloody spoor as it fled to the south, disappearing behind the bushes along the riverbank.

Police dogs have been on the scent, but my arm has given a raised finger to all attempts at capture, an insolent gesture, my friends will know, it did not learn from me.

Nurses drew off blood to check my DNA. An army of volunteers, recruited worldwide, now seek a suitable donor arm.

I've decided that I will accept any suitable arm of reasonable length. I will not be keen for friends to know me by the soubriquet Wingy.

It will be cold tonight. I do wish my arm would come home.

Beware the DOONHAMER VARIANT.

Doonhamer is the well-known nickname for a Dumfries resident.

A peculiarity of the Irish Republic's Covid-19 vaccination roll out has emerged, signalling that present vaccines do not protect against all exceptions. Both male and female vaccine recipients have developed a deep-seated cunnilingus obsession. Observers first noticed the stricken, out on a minge-munching hunt, in a small Irish border town.

Beware THE MUFF VARIANT!

The knowledge isn't well known, outside a certain Scottish football club boardroom, of the mass Covid-19 vaccination of the first team squad. However, the vaccinations have backfired big-time. Immunology professors, mainly resident in Western Glasgow, state categorically that the club player's catastrophic dip in goal scoring abilities, from early in the 20/21 footballing season, in their league and in international matches, is wholly attributable to major alterations in the DNA of the vaccine injected.

Immunology professors have issued a warning to other Scottish football clubs: BEWARE THE TENLENNONINAROW VARIANT vaccine.

Since the Covid19 virus first infected humans, immunologists thought animals were immune to the virus. However, veterinarians have noticed that this is no longer true; swabs from the cheeks of animals and observed signs have proved them infected.

Vets have noticed a symptom that affects male dogs: the unexplainable, shrinking vertebrae syndrome. The osteoporosis is reducing body elasticity along the spine length.

Animal welfare organisations have issued this warning:

Beware The BALLSLESSLICKED, canine variant.

A woman's association, The League of Independent Bitches, or LIB, for short, cruising Orkney, aboard a chartered yacht, landed on a beach near Birsay, in a dinghy. The women, keen to explore the intriguing flora and fauna of the islands, overnighted in a bothy further inland, close by a well-known village.

Next morning, on arising, each woman discovered the overnight development of enlarged vaginal labia. One disturbed woman, describing the transformation unenthusiastically, hollered, 'I've got piss flaps like fucking saddlebags. It's the fucking virus!'

Beware the TWATT VARIANT.

Areas of Germany are without supplies of any of the Covid-19 virus vaccines, due to any one of the various reasons quoted in the media. In the Bavarian Alps, where a particular mountain and a small town share the same evocative name, the virus has mutated. Youths of the town, and those living on the mountain, who have contracted the mutation, stand out. On any street corner, shop doorway, play-park or ski slope, locals see young males masturbieren and the girls klitoral stimulierend.

Local TV stations broadcast this thoughtful message: VORSICHT VOR DER WANK VARIANTE

Doctors report a bed wetting side effect amongst Covid-19 vaccine recipients. Concerned mothers and wives, resident in many of Scotland's central belt communities, centring on Craigneuk, are losing sleep worrying about overnight drownings.

Beware the PISHYWISHY VARIANT.

The Covid-19 vaccine roll out, on a major island off the Eastern Canada mainland, has accelerated since the turn of the year. However, the vaccine used did not protect against all abnormalities, as a small town population have discovered.

Peculiarities in behaviour were first noticed when town females, of the ages 80 to 90, took to the streets, in droves, naked, hollering, like moose in the rutting season, the word, Strapadicktome.'

Street corner druggists, sensing a window in the market, dropped their usual wares and began touting the back-street drug Trydixagin.

Town elders have added a notice to the signboard that confirms its sister city, Hollywood, lies 5483km to the south.

Visitors should BEWARE THE DILDO VARIANT.

The European Union's tardy rollout of the Covid-19 vaccine, forced Civic Elders to modify the historic and popular name of their Austrian village.

Founded in the 6th Century AD, by the Bavarian nobleman Focko, world tourists today deviate on their European leg to visit the village for photo-shoots and selfies at the famous naming sign. The village identifier stood, in tourist interest, alongside that of the German town of Wank, the Newfoundland town of Dildo and the Irish town of Muff.

Villagers, testing Covid-19 positive for the mutation rife in the area, experienced pronunciation difficulties and could not articulate the ck when uttering the village name.

Civic Elders had an alternative solution and acted quickly: the ck had to go; the simpler for villagers to get their Teutonic tongue around gg, would replace the troublesome ck.

Today, the signpost does not show the old name, but the concocted version, FUGGING

Tourist brochures now contain the warning: BEWARE THE FUCKING VARIANT.